CHRISTMAS IN DIXIE

A SWEET SOUTHERN ROMANTIC COMEDY

KACI LANE

CHRISTMAS IN DIXIE

CHAPTER ONE

Lacie

"With a cold front moving in Christmas Eve, it looks like Atlanta might just get a white Christmas. So keep an eye on the roads. I'm Lacie Sanderson, on location in downtown Atlanta, wishing you all a safe holiday."

I put on the smile that helped me win Apple Sauce Queen my junior year of high school and wait for Dustin's signal. After an awkward minute, he nods, and the camera light stops blinking.

"That's a wrap, Lacie."

I immediately slump my shoulders and relax my quivering cheeks. "Thank God, it's freezing out here." That came out a little too southern, as does most everything I say when the camera isn't rolling.

"Well, you're headed west. Mark said the precipitation should fizzle out before it reaches Alabama."

I arch my eyebrow at Dustin. "No, it's going to move

faster than Mark thinks. Alabama will have snow by Christmas morning, if not sooner."

Dustin shakes his head and chuckles. "Whatever you say, Lacie Bug."

I frown. He'll never let me live down the day my parents visited The Weather Channel and spilled the beans on my childhood nickname.

Dustin continues packing up his camera as I remove my earpiece. Once everything is put away in the news van, he wishes me a Merry Christmas and heads back toward the station.

I blow into my chapped hands and hop in my Honda CR-V. I turn on the heater and choose my favorite Christmas music station. It's only a few miles to my apartment, but it takes a half hour thanks to all the rush-hour traffic running both ways. I assume half the people are headed to work and the other half out of town. Over the past few years, I've met very few people in Atlanta who are actually from Atlanta.

After witnessing an exchange of horn honks and obscene gestures among my fellow commuters, I make it home. I've got to finish packing and make sure everything is in order so I can leave after seeing Collins. My insides warm, and I smile. Not the fake Apple Sauce Queen smile I reserve for on-camera, but my natural, not-so-over-the-top smile. Collins and I met on New Year's Eve last year and have dated ever since.

He checks off all my boxes. He's handsome, successful, smart, and compassionate, and he's been going to church with me. I can totally see us getting married one day. Which is why I've made every excuse under the sun to keep him away from my family.

As my G-Maw would say, they'd have him running like a chicken with his head cut off.

In high school, my daddy strategically cleaned his guns at

the dining room table whenever a new guy would pick me up for a date. And he still says he can't understand why I broke up with Bradley. Ugh. From leading our high school football team to win state to serving as the Apple Cart County sheriff, Bradley Manning has made the whole town of Wisteria, Alabama, practically worship him.

I roll my eyes as I hop out of my crossover and lock the door behind me. Daddy is the least of my worries. My extended family is the real reason I want to keep Collins under wraps until I lock him down.

I go inside my apartment and take a whiff of the air. I should probably wash my egg skillet soiling in the sink before I leave. When you have to get to work before six a.m., you learn to let a few things slide.

I drop my purse on the tiny kitchen counter and roll up my coat sleeves. As I scrub the yellow scales on my not-so-nonstick skillet, my mind wanders. I imagine walking down the aisle toward Collins in a beautiful gown, with my arm looped through Daddy's. Then my perfect day is ruined by my crazy Aunt Misty whistling loudly and bringing everyone's attention to her improper choice of wedding attire.

I wince as I rinse the pan. Yeah, we're definitely eloping. With any luck, I can keep Collins away from the full Mayberry clan at least until the ink on our marriage license dries. Then it will be too late for him to cut and run, as G-Maw would say.

I reach for my hand towel that reads, "Christmas Cookies and Hallmark Movies." I dry my hands, then spread the towel across the counter and set the pan on top to dry. The hand towel takes up half my counter space.

When I moved to Atlanta, my choices were get a teeny tiny apartment or a roommate. And since I knew absolutely nobody and I'm not claustrophobic, I chose Option A. I'm not a huge fan of the city, but working for The Weather

Channel has been my dream since fourth grade, when Jim Vann visited our school.

In Alabama, we have a weird hierarchy of celebrities. There's Nick Saban, the Alabama football coach, followed by two heavyset guys who have a radio show about little more than food and corny impersonations. Then there's Jim Vann. He's the king of weather in the southeast.

I've watched him navigate us through every storm throughout my life. I've always had a fascination with weather, but when he visited my elementary school and showed us weather graphs and polygons in real time, I made up my mind then and there to become a weather girl. But not just any weather girl. I wanted to anchor the news for The Weather Channel. And with an on-camera position in the field, I'm well on my way to fulfilling that dream.

I remove my coat and lay it across my purse, then head to my bedroom. My suitcase is already open on the bed, with most of my clothing folded beside it. I walk to my closet and stand on my toes to rummage through the top shelf. Or more like the only shelf. If I don't take my own coveralls, I'll end up wearing my brother's skanky hunting clothes to the family hog killing.

As soon as I smoosh my coveralls in the corner of my suitcase, I change out of my work clothes. The last thing I want to do is wear slacks, heels, and a blouse on a four-hour drive to the middle of nowhere, so I exchange that outfit for my thickest sweatshirt and some yoga pants.

I check my appearance in the full-length mirror hanging from my closet door. There. A bulky Mississippi State sweatshirt to make my brother mad, along with slightly faded elastic-waist pants. The perfect attire for Wisteria.

Collins

MY STOMACH CHURNS as I get a text from Lacie saying she's done packing and ready for me to come over. I text back that I'm on my way and stare down at my own suitcase in the hallway.

She has no idea that I've managed to take off work and spend Christmas with her. I shrug on my jacket and slip out into the garage before my roommates ask any questions. They know I'm planning on visiting her family for the holidays, but they don't know my intentions.

I've known Charlie since rush week at Georgia, and he's sending vibes that he knows something is up. But I can't tell him or Mitch that I've had a diamond burning a hole in my pocket for several weeks now. Mitch would try and talk me out of marriage, as he's committed to nothing but noncommitment. And Charlie would act awkward around Lacie, since his weakness is keeping things on the DL.

I run a hand across my short beard and hop into my Land Rover. I feel a little silly dressed in scrubs, knowing I'm coming back here after leaving Lacie's. But she thinks I'm on call this weekend and that I'm going to the hospital after I leave her place. Lacie picks up on everything, which has made keeping secrets from her much harder than fooling the two goobers I live with.

We both live downtown, but I would like to buy a house in the suburbs once we marry. I know Lacie's only in Atlanta for work, and having a yard wider than my push mower might be a nice change of pace.

It doesn't take me long to get to her apartment building. I jump out and knock on the door. She answers right away and smiles up at me, her chocolate-brown eyes shining. I step inside and pull her in for a hug. She's warm and cozy and smells like flowers. I'm not sure what kind, but it's soothing. I've dozed off more than once on her couch while she snuggled up to me with her hair under my nose.

We both work crazy hours, but that's part of the commonality that kicked off our very first conversation. And her drive and ambition were a total turn-on from day one. Then her sweet-as-molasses voice sent me over the edge. It didn't take but a few months for me to know I wanted to marry that girl one day.

Lacie lifts her head and gives me a quick kiss before breaking the hug. I follow her a few steps to her tiny living room and take a seat on the couch. She plops down beside me. "Maybe you won't have to go in on Christmas Day," she says.

I shrug. With any luck, we'll be snuggled up at her parents' house celebrating our first Christmas engaged. "There's a good chance I will. I'm still the low man on the totem pole in surgery."

"Well, as someone who had to give a weather update at every fake Santa stationed in Atlanta last year, I can assure you working on Christmas isn't fun."

"But you had such a cheerful attitude doing it." I run my hand through her dark hair and smile.

"You didn't know me last Christmas."

"Not in person. But I still watched the weather." It was true. When I saw her at the hospital benefit on New Year's Eve, I knew right away she was the beautiful girl I'd watched deliver the weather every morning while getting ready for work.

Lacie leans back against my chest and sighs. "I'm gonna miss you this week."

"Yeah, and I'll miss you." I try to sound as if I'm not about to strike out toward Wisteria.

Lacie never says much about her hometown, except that it's small and she has a big family. It's probably one of those places with a gazebo downtown and Christmas wreaths on every streetlamp. Like in those low-budget Christmas movies I've suffered through the past month, all because I love her.

She raises her head and grins at me. "I better hit the road. The temperature is supposed to drop all day."

I chuckle and pull her close. "And you can't drive in the cold?"

She narrows her eyes at me. "No, it's gonna snow."

I laugh harder. "Okay, maybe here."

"No, in Alabama, too."

"Uh-huh." I nod my head.

She gives me the same face ornery patients do when I try and convince them that residents are real doctors. "Collins, I've been studying the weather patterns for Alabama all week. Trust me."

"Okay, babe." I raise my palms in surrender.

She stands slowly and reaches out her hand. I take it and stand in front of her, wrapping my arms around her small waist and pulling her in for a kiss. She fits perfectly between my arms, and all I can think about is how I can't wait to officially spend the rest of my life snuggled next to her.

After the kiss, I squeeze her in tighter, feeling her heart beat against my chest. It's all I can stand to not go ahead and propose right here, in her living room, while she's dressed in sweats and I'm in my scrubs.

But Lacie deserves better than that. She's old-fashioned and high-class. I need to meet her parents before I propose and let them know my intentions. Then I need to plan the perfect proposal. Someplace outside. Heck, maybe even in a gazebo. Someplace special, where she'll always remember that moment.

After a long minute, I pull away, knowing she's anxious to get on the road. "I'll put your bags in for you."

"Thanks."

I follow her to the door, where she has way too many bags for a few nights. But she always overpacks. I've never understood that. I could go to the moon with only one suitcase.

I take her two biggest bags, and she follows me with a fancy duffle and her purse. I maneuver them all to fit best in the back of her crossover and close the hatch. She smiles and kisses me gently on the lips.

I smile back. "Merry Christmas, Lacie."

"I'll be sure to call you when I get there. Wisteria doesn't have the best cell service, so I'll call from Mama's. You'll have the house number that way, too."

I nod. "I love you."

"I love you, too." Her eyes sparkle as those words leave her pink lips. My heart skips a beat, and it takes everything in me to not jump in her vehicle and suggest we elope.

Instead, I run my hand down her hair and squeeze her cheek. Then I go to my own vehicle and drive back home. By now, my roommates are on their way to work, so I can get packed and head toward Wisteria.

My hand trembles as I fumble with fitting my key into the garage door. I'm going to a place I've only heard about, with no real plan of how or exactly when I'll propose. I'm thinking Christmas Eve, but the lack of certainty behind it all makes my mouth go dry. It's not like me to not have a plan.

I go inside and change out of my scrubs and into khaki pants and a buttoned shirt. My usual look outside of work. Then I get to packing.

After stacking my clothes and tossing in my toiletries bag, I fumble around the bottom of my sock drawer. There. I bring out the tiny black box and pop it open. The corners of my mouth raise as I admire my grandmother's diamond. As the only child and grandchild, she left it to me for my future bride. I've already had it sized to fit Lacie, thanks to sneaking one of her rings to the jeweler's.

I close the lid and exhale a huge breath. Then I tuck the box securely in the inside zipper pocket of my suitcase. I take a quick glance around my room to make sure I didn't miss anything, then head outside.

As I climb into the driver's seat, a knot forms in my stomach. I'm about to drive hours away to a town I have no idea about to meet people I've only seen in photos, then propose to the woman I love. But if it ends with Lacie promising to be my wife, it will all be more than worth it.

CHAPTER TWO

Lacie

I suck down the last of my Starbucks and turn up my favorite Christmas song. I'm now in Tuscaloosa, so it shouldn't be long before I get to Apple Cart County.

I laugh at how before moving to Atlanta, I complained about Tuscaloosa traffic. But I drive straight through town, no problem. Of course, football season is over, which makes all the difference in T-town. As I drive farther, large office buildings and interstates change into neighborhoods and smaller shops. Then the houses become scattered among hay fields and pine trees. Once all the restaurants switch from fast food chains to little cafes, I know I'm getting close.

My stomach pits with the same conflicted feeling that plagues every trip back to Wisteria. I love my parents and grandparents. And I mostly love my little brother. I also enjoy the slower pace of small-town life. However, there's a price to pay for all that. I can't manage to stay more than one day without my crazy aunt popping up. And even a trip to Dollar General to buy toothpaste turns into an interrogation by whatever gossiping granny is in line beside me. I've learned the hard way to pack everything I might ever need—and multiples of it—to avoid an emergency DG run.

My insides warm as I spot the orchard at the end of Apple Cart, the neighboring—and slightly larger—small town to mine. Apple Cart is the county seat, and the town is well kept, with more stores. Granted, there's still a ton of colorful characters and interesting places. There's even a general store that's like a combo of new clothes and yard-sale crap. But compared to Wisteria, Apple Cart looks like the cover of *Southern Living*.

I think my town is the only one to have a hotel, liquor store, and Mexican restaurant all in the same building, under the same management. Well, technically it sits right across the county line, since Apple Cart is a dry county. But the mailing address is Wisteria. Lucky us.

Downtown Apple Cart is nicely decorated, with fake snowflakes on all the streetlamps. Even the Piggly Wiggly has a blowup Santa on the roof. He waves a little too wildly as I pass by. Must be the cold-front winds coming this way.

The ten-year-old inside of me gets a little giddy at the thought of a white Christmas. Nobody believes it's coming to Alabama, not even my boss. But I've studied the weather patterns for over a week, and I wouldn't be surprised if Jim Vann confirmed my predictions on tonight's local news.

I drive into the Wisteria town limits and notice that our welcome sign is now held up via PVC pipes. Great. Quality tourist advertisement there. At least the sign is legible. Or maybe that's not such a good thing.

The drive through town takes all of two minutes. There's a wooden manger scene in front of my parents' church, and lights strung on city hall. Not much more. But I didn't expect Dollar General and the gas station to decorate.

A few minutes later, I turn down the first paved road since leaving town. Most of my family lives on this road. And only my family. It's a dead end that leads to endless pine trees, where my family hunts. Legend has it that my grandpa won a hundred acres in a poker match back in the late 1950s. He built a long, straight road, and then his modest house at the beginning of it. That way, he could watch whoever came onto his property. Later on, both my parents and my aunt and uncle cleared land and built on the road. So now all my grandparents' kids live here. Well, except for Aunt Misty.

She's moved around a lot, but surprisingly never got any farther than ten miles from my grandparents. I'm not sure where she lives now. At one time, she had a trailer beside my grandparents' house. Then she remarried, sold the trailer, and moved toward Apple Cart with her husband. But that was a few husbands ago, so I'm not sure where she's living now.

I pass my grandparents' house and Woody's RV. He's a family friend who's recently divorced. G-Paw let him hook his RV up where Misty's trailer once sat.

A minute later, I pull up to my parents' log home. I park my vehicle and relax my shoulders. Before I can unbuckle my seat belt, the front door flies open and my mama bounces down the front porch steps.

I unbuckle and open my door in time for her to wrap around me. "My baby," she says. I pat her back and exhale once she releases me from an impressively tight grip for a woman her size.

"I'm so glad you're here. Are you hungry?"

"Actually . . ." I stare at the plastic cup with stained frappuccino remains. "What do you have?"

Mama grins, showing off her perfect teeth. If someone were to put her in heels and a flowered apron, she'd make the perfect Stepford wife. "I made a pot of vegetable soup last night, and I have some Christmas candy. Your brother ate all the leftover cornbread."

"Of course, he did." I frown, then laugh. I need to monitor my comfort-food intake anyway. I don't want to return to Atlanta looking all fluffy on camera.

Mama loops her arm through mine and leads me to the house. I glance back at my Honda.

"Oh, I'll make the boys bring in your things when they come in."

I nod my head. I don't even have to ask where they are, since they hunt and shoot guns every spare minute that both my dad is off work and my brother is home from college.

The whole house is decorated like a winter wonderland. Mama is obsessed with Christmas trees and has one in every room, including the hunting tree in the basement. I follow her into the kitchen and pick a seat where I won't knock into the John Deere tree by the window.

"I can't wait for you to see all my trees lit up at night. I've upgraded some of them and added one to the back deck."

"No kidding." I laugh. The John Deere one started as a tabletop tree. Then my dad convinced her to move it to the floor since he couldn't find the salt and pepper easily. I guess she wanted a larger one to fill the space.

Mama brings me a bowl of warm soup and a cup of sweet tea, then sits beside me.

"Thanks."

She smiles. "I'm just so happy you're home. Last year was so sad with you working."

I smile. "Yeah. I've finally been there long enough to pull a little rank on some people and take vacation."

"That's wonderful, honey. I love seeing your pretty face on TV. You're like our own little Wisteria celebrity around here."

I blow my soup, then raise an eyebrow at her. "Really?"

"Oh, yes. Just last month, Betty Sue and Fred got cable TV because they're tired of never being able to see you."

"That sounds extreme. You know they can watch me online." I take a bite of my soup and close my eyes as the warm concoction hits my throat. To sound cliché, there really is nothing like a home-cooked meal.

"Well, they can't do the online."

I bite my tongue to keep from laughing. Despite being educated and a professional, my mom overuses "the." "The Walmart" is her favorite. But at least she doesn't pluralize every place. That habit belongs to G-Paw.

"Why can't they go online? I thought you guys got internet out here a few years back."

"We did, but they're too old for computers."

"Aren't they like sixty?"

"Exactly." Mama widens her pretty eyes.

I continue eating my soup, fighting the urge to comment that they only have a decade on her. She stands and circles the kitchen island. I watch as she rummages through a Tupperware. She returns with a paper plate full of assorted candies.

"Earl Ed will be at G-Maw and G-Paw's this year."

"Don't tell me. Bradley's escorting him." My first cousin went to jail ten years ago. He was the local mail carrier for a main route in town, and people started complaining about missing their mail. Ironically, it was just Netflix DVDs and Victoria's Secret catalogues. They traced it back to Earl Ed and searched his apartment. Sure enough, he'd been reselling the DVDs. And I don't even want to think about what he did with the catalogues.

"No, he doesn't even have an ankle bracelet now. He's out on parole. Earl and Carla are hoping since everything's going to the online now he can stay clean."

"Well." I try not to roll my eyes, and bite into a chocolate-covered something. It's almonds and cashews. "Wow, I like this. Pinterest?"

"No, Pioneer Woman."

I nod. "Show me how to make it before I go."

"Don't worry, we'll have to make more. Your brother discovered them last night.

Now I do roll my eyes.

"Oh, and Michael met a girl."

I widen my eyes and reach for a haystack. "Good for him." Michael is Aunt Misty's oldest kid. Anyone who doesn't know us well assumes he's my Uncle Earl's son, and that Earl Ed is Aunt Misty's. "Who is she?"

Mama shakes her head. "I don't know. We're supposed to meet her this week. She's from Mississippi."

"Huh, I wonder if she went to State."

Mama smiles. "Maybe so."

I polish off the last bite of my peanut-butter-smothered pretzels and wipe my mouth. I stare at the plate of sweets and lick my lips. Then I envision myself going back to work like Tim Allen on *The Santa Clause*. That's enough to make me push the plate back.

I sip my tea and stare out the window. I can't wait until the snow gets here. Something about growing up in the deep south, where its warm ninety percent of the time, and my fascination with all things weather makes snow an extra treat for me.

"Baby, if you want to, you can go rest a while. I'll make the boys get everything out of your car. Then later, we can cook."

"Okay, thanks." I stand and hug Mama as I pass her. "I love you."

She pats my back. "I love you, too."

I leave the kitchen and retreat to my childhood bedroom,

which is still covered in pictures from high school. I laugh at my Apple Sauce Queen sash draped across a trophy on my dresser. Then I reach for the phone by my bed. I untangle the massive cord enough to pull it from the receiver and call Collins.

Collins

I PULL up to a gas station near Birmingham. According to my GPS, I've got a little more than an hour's drive to Wisteria. I get out and stretch my back and legs before pumping gas. After yawning so wide that my jaw pops, I decide I need a Mountain Dew to finish my trip.

A few minutes ago, Lacie called to tell me she'd made it to her parents' house. That was a huge relief, since I left not long after her. My skin tingles as I imagine sitting across a living room from her parents, who've never met me before.

After my gas tank is full, I walk inside for something caffeinated to refill my personal tank. A large plastic Santa wearing an Alabama football jersey greets me as I open the door. I go to the cooler and find the largest Mountain Dew available, then head toward the counter. The cashier's front teeth are gray, and she asks in a husky voice if I'd like any cigarettes.

"No thank you."

"You sure?" She coughs. "We're running a sale on the unfiltered ones."

"No thanks, I'm good." I force a smile as I insert my card into the slot and wait for it to process. She grins back. I wonder how many she smokes a day to stain her teeth that much. Maybe she gets an employee discount on top of the sale.

Once the scanner beeps, I pull my card out and hightail it back to the Land Rover. But not without almost knocking over Santa in the process. He lets out a gruff "ho, ho, ho," as if he's running out of batteries.

I shake my head and continue on my journey. Even though I grew up in Georgia, I'm not too familiar with the state of Alabama. I've been to Tuscaloosa, Birmingham, and the beach. That's about it. And I've never seen a sign for Wisteria anytime we traveled toward the coast.

My GPS continues spouting out directions, interrupting my classic-rock playlist whenever there's a turn. I know I'm getting farther out of civilization when the four lanes end and the directions tell me to stay straight for a good many miles.

I continue driving as I nurse my Mountain Dew and toss around ways I might introduce myself to Lacie's parents. Should I say I'm a surgeon or a resident? Or simply a doctor? Or should I not mention my profession at all? Most people would love to have their daughter date a doctor. But I don't want to come off as conceited.

I tap my thumbs on the steering wheel, debating my approach. That's when I realize that after dating almost a year, I know nothing about Lacie's family. I know their names, and that her mom does something at the University of Alabama and her dad works in a mine. And I have seen their photos, but that's it. I have no idea what they like and dislike or how they live. She never talks about them.

I exhale and take another sip of my drink. Liquid courage. At least, I hope. That's about the strongest thing I have nowadays, as Lacie doesn't like alcohol. Plus, there's the whole problem of getting calls to go into the hospital at random hours of the night. That will put a damper on your social life.

There's a huge patch of apple trees on my right, and I haven't seen a store I recognize in the last half hour. A quick glance at my phone lets me know I'm close. My GPS sends me away from the major highway and funnels me toward a traffic light. I take a left and meet a small hill, with two apple trees surrounding a sign that reads, "Welcome to Apple Cart."

I drive through town, which is a mixture of the picturesque small towns seen in movies and people hanging out in a Piggly Wiggly parking lot in their pajamas. Very strange.

The town only lasts a few miles, then I'm rolling past cotton fields and a sign that reads, "Gamers Paradise." Must be some sort of video arcade. I stay straight ahead like the GPS says, and I end up at a sign for Wisteria. Unlike the white wood Apple Cart sign, this one is white plastic poles with scratches across the word. My gut tightens, and I hope this isn't a bad omen.

I continue driving, passing only a gas station and a dollar store before I'm back to just houses. About that time, my GPS starts spinning. I swallow hard and check my phone service. It's nonexistent.

Just great. I know Lacie's address, but I have no idea where to find it. Is it the dirt road to my left or the gravel road on my right? Or have I already passed it? I slow down to read the signs. Then I pull out the atlas from my glove compartment. I'm going old school. My grandpa would be so proud.

Wouldn't you know it—Wisteria isn't even on the map. Let alone the streets of this place. There's a tiny dot for Apple Cart, and that's it.

The county outline is small itself, making Tuscaloosa and

Jefferson counties look like they're on steroids by comparison. I sigh and chew my nails. My thumb nail is already to the quick, but somehow I manage to bite off more.

I toss the atlas toward the passenger seat and notice that I'm now in the middle of the road. Good thing there is zero traffic. It's like I'm Rick Grimes driving into town after the apocalypse.

And that's about what this feels like with no phone service and not a building in sight. I'm craning my neck at every side road, in anticipation that I'll hear banjos playing any minute.

Instead, I hear a police siren. Perfect. Just what I need.

I groan and pull over to the side of the road. The cop pulls up behind me, his lights dancing wildly. A guy my age gets out and adjusts a tan cowboy hat. I stand corrected. *He* is Rick Grimes. Except with a sharp jaw and broad shoulders.

I slump back in my seat and roll down my window. The scent of cheap weed seeps into my vehicle. What the . . .?

I hop out and meet him at my door. "Officer . . ." I read his badge before I continue. "Bradley, that is not my weed you smell."

He gives me a confused face. I curse myself under my breath for saying anything.

"Excuse me?"

"I was talking to myself." Now my hands are sweating. "But don't you smell that?"

He sniffs the air, then bursts out laughing. "You mean the dead skunk in that ditch?" He points a few feet behind my Land Rover. Sure enough, it's an actual skunk, not skunk weed.

"We don't allow that kind of hippy crap around here. Neither do we allow drinking and driving. What have you had to drink?"

"A Mountain Dew. And a cappuccino earlier."

"Right . . . I'm gonna need you to walk this line." He points to the line on the edge of the road. I stand on it and walk it perfectly.

Still not satisfied, he shines a flashlight at my eyeballs.

"Ouch." I blink.

"Your pupils are dilated."

"Well, yeah, you shined a light in them."

He narrows his eyes, not happy with my rebuttal. "I'll be right back." He comes back with a breathalyzer. Only after my results show a zero alcohol level does he back off. "So, if you're not drunk and you're not on skunk, why were you drivin' all loopy like?"

"I'm trying to find Mayberry Road, and my GPS cut out a few miles back. I've never been to Wisteria before."

"Well, that's evident. Might I ask what you want on Mayberry Road?"

"Lacie."

His mouth opens the slightest bit, but he stays silent, so I continue.

"Lacie Sanderson. Do you know her?"

He scratches his chin and grins. "Yeah, I know her."

"We're dating, and I'm going to surprise her for Christmas."

His grin widens. "*You're* dating Lacie?"

"Yes," I answer slowly, hoping this will be his last nonsense question.

He starts laughing and slaps me on the shoulder. "Why didn't you say so? I'll take you there."

"Oh, well thanks."

"Don't mention it. Follow me." He starts back toward his car. I hear him mumble to himself, "*He's* dating Lacie." Then he laughs again before getting behind the wheel.

I get in my own vehicle and wait for him to pull in front of me. We drive a few more miles, then he turns off his lights and puts on his blinker. We turn down a paved road with a camper at the end. After passing the camper and an older home, we pull up to a log house that would fit in well in Gatlinburg.

Bradley gets out and slams his door. "Here we are."

I follow him to the front door. A moment after we knock, a man answers.

"Bradley." The man shakes Bradley's hand, then pulls him in for a side hug, not noticing I'm there. "Come in, son."

"Thanks, Mr. Sanderson. I rescued this young man on his way here."

"Oh." Lacie's dad notices me for the first time and extends his hand. "Joey Sanderson."

"Nice to meet you, Joey, I'm Collins."

His eyes widen. "So, you're Collins." He glances at Bradley, then back at me. "And it's Mr. Sanderson, please."

My ears heat up. Most people where I'm from don't like for a man my age to call them Mr. or Mrs., my patients included. I nod, then turn my attention elsewhere to try and ease the awkwardness. An array of deer heads and turkeys cover the wall above the fireplace.

"Bradley." A younger guy comes up and does some random handshake with him. The kind middle school football players might do before a game for luck.

"Hey, Liam. How's Auburn?"

"Same ole, same ole. I got a new gun last week."

"Sweet. What kind?"

They start talking words I don't understand about calibers and scopes. This leaves me in silence beside Mr. Sanderson. My mouth goes dry, and I cough.

Either he senses my uneasiness or he's uneasy, too, because he quickly says, "Lacie's in the kitchen." Then, without looking my way, he starts walking. I follow him into the kitchen.

Sure enough, there's Lacie standing by the sink with her mom, stirring something.

"Hey, Lacie." She looks up when I speak. But she isn't smiling. Instead, her face goes pale and her mouth drops.

That's when I realize that she isn't looking at me. She's staring behind me at Bradley.

CHAPTER THREE

Lacie

I blink to make sure this isn't a dream. Nope, it's a nightmare. My current boyfriend, whom I've managed to shield from Wisteria for almost a year, is standing in my parents' kitchen. And right behind him is my high school and college boyfriend, whom I've managed to avoid for almost a year.

Have I had a few thoughts about Bradley since our breakup? Some what ifs and why nots? Sure. But not since I started dating Collins. Now, they're both here to witness me dressed like a slob, with my hair in a messy bun, makeup smudged from an hour-plus nap. Just peachy.

"What are you doing here?"

Both of them answer simultaneously. I hold my finger up in front of Bradley. Although I'm confused as to why he's here also, I really couldn't give a rat's rear end, as G-Maw would say.

"I wanted to surprise you for Christmas. I got off work the next few days," Collins says.

My eyes widen enough that I feel my hairline raising. "Oh." I smile. Part of me is thrilled to spend our first Christmas as a couple together. The other part wants to warn him to run before Bradley or Daddy or Liam ruins it. And if he makes it past that many levels of Wisteria, there's always Aunt Misty. She's like the monster in the castle on the final level of all those old Nintendo games.

"Well, Collins, it's a pleasure to finally meet you." Mama wipes her hands on her apron, steps forward, and hugs him. I let out a breath, thankful for her saving the day.

Meanwhile, Bradley stands there like he's patrolling our kitchen. I shoot him a mean look. He shrugs.

I set the mixing bowl I'm holding on the counter and roll down my sweatshirt sleeves. "Collins, I'll go help you get your luggage."

"Nonsense, your daddy can do that." Mama gives us her own beauty queen smile.

"Let him do it, he's a grown man," Daddy spouts out from the corner of the kitchen in between bites of peanut brittle.

"Of course." Collins turns and walks out of the house.

As soon as he's out of earshot, I cross my arms. "Daddy, that was rude."

"Sorry, Lacie Bug. I just call it like I see it."

I roll my eyes, then turn to Bradley. "And what are you doing here?"

"I escorted him. He was crawling down the road lost as a sinner, because his GPS wouldn't work."

I exhale through my nostrils. "Well, thanks for that, but you're free to go back to whatever it was you were doing."

"You mean protecting our county?" Bradley's dark eyes narrow.

"Sure, whatever, Barney Fife."

Bradley tips his hat and frowns at me. "Always a pleasure, Lacie."

I turn toward the sink and grab my bowl, stirring the cake batter so hard that my wrist starts to throb. I don't turn back around until I hear boots on the wood floor. When I do, Liam and Bradley are gone.

"Don't be hard on Bradley."

I slam the bowl on the counter, sending some chocolate drops to the granite. "Daddy, why do you always take up for him?"

Daddy shrugs. "He's a good guy. He can't help it Collin got lost."

"It's Collins, Daddy."

"That's plural."

"Yes, I know. It's a family name. Just like Earl Ed was named after Uncle Earl and G-Paw."

"Well, Earl Ed isn't plural."

I slam my hand on the counter and prop my other hand on my hip. "Well, if you write it out, it's past tense."

Mama smirks. "Joey, she does have a point." I nod at Daddy.

Daddy shakes his head. "Fine, I'm sorry. I can't help that I like Bradley. I'll play nice with Collin or Collins, or whatever."

I clinch my teeth at Daddy's backhanded apology. Knowing that's all I'll get from him, I respond, "Thank you, Daddy."

A few minutes later, Collins comes back into the kitchen rolling a suitcase. He stops in front of the island and parks the bag by his feet.

"Bradley just invited Lacie and me to ride with him in the Apple Cart Christmas parade."

"You said no, right?" My nerves tick as I anticipate his response.

"I actually said yes. I thought that was nice of him."

"I told you he's a nice guy." Daddy nods at me.

I ignore Daddy and answer Collins instead. "Aren't you tired from driving all day? I think we'd have more fun staying in and watching movies."

"Now, that's not true." Mama pouts. "The parade will be a great way for Collins to meet everyone and get a feel of the town."

I bite my tongue to keep from protesting. As much as I disagree with my mom right now, what she says gives me an idea. Maybe if Collins sees downtown Apple Cart, he will be satisfied and not care to hang out in downtown Wisteria. He's always saying how he wants to see where I grew up. If I have to show him Apple Cart or Wisteria, I'm all for picking the lesser of two evils.

Mama, Daddy, and Collins all stare at me like they're dogs and I have a bag of bacon strips. I can't help but make one more rebuttal. "Collins, we don't have to go unless you want to."

"I think it would be fun to see the town. I've never been to a small-town parade before, much less rode in one."

I nod slowly, and Mama claps her hands. "I'll take plenty of pictures for you kids. This will be perfect for his first visit."

Daddy grins around a mouthful of candy. Most likely, his amusement comes from me having to ride with Bradley. I take a step back from the cake batter and sit on a stool at the island. I think I'm gonna be sick.

Collins

MY FIRST FEW hours in Wisteria were interesting. First, I got pulled over for supposed drunkenness, followed by a police escort to Lacie's house. Then, in a desperate attempt to find some common ground with Mr. Sanderson, I asked about one of the deer heads on the wall. This led to an hour-long story of how he tracked the deer for two days before killing it.

I finally had a few moments alone with Lacie before we had to get ready for the parade, when she helped me settle into the basement. Of course, our alone time was cut short by her mother coming in and out with bedding and other things I might need. Not to mention her brother coming in and out for guns every fifteen minutes.

Now I'm about to witness the Apple Cart County parade.

Mr. Sanderson pulls into a gravel parking lot and stops in front of a metal building. A sign beneath the larger "General Store" sign reads, "From a cradle to a coffin." A little freaky, if you ask me.

Everyone gets out, so I follow. As if right on cue, Bradley drives up on a John Deere tractor. It has a cedar branch wreath on the front and Christmas lights around it. "Glad you guys could make it. Hop on."

He has to be kidding. There's one seat beside him. Well, more like one half of a seat.

"We can't all fit on that," Lacie protests. That's my girl.

"Sure we can. Collins can sit in the buddy seat, and you can sit on my lap."

Bradley seems like a nice enough guy, but this is a little over the top. "I don't think that's a good idea," I say.

"Why, you think it would work better if you sat on my lap?"

Mr. Sanderson laughs behind me. I try my best to ignore him.

"Why can't she and I share that little seat?"

"No offense, but it's barely on there as it is. Two adults will break it."

I inhale, then exhale and lower my shoulders. "I'll sit on the side."

"Okay, glad you agree."

Without saying a word, I climb up the step and get on the fender. "This side."

Lacie smiles at me and sits in the tiny seat, not Bradley's lap. I lift my chin in a metaphorical "take that" toward Bradley. If we were animals in a jungle, I'd roar, but no sense in causing a scene in front of some warehouse coffin building.

I grip onto the edge of the fender as Bradley rolls out across the gravel parking lot. Dozens of floats and cars and even horses are lined up in a row. We bypass them and park in front of the high school bands. An ATV with a sign on the front that reads "Sheriff Bradley Manning, Grand Marshall" pulls in front of us. It's driven by a kid in a Santa hat.

I squirm against the hard metal beneath my khakis to try and not sit on a strand of Christmas lights.

"Collins, if you want, you can ride behind Riley on the four-wheeler."

I flare my nostrils and try not to sound gruff with my response. "No thanks, Bradley, I'm good."

"If you say so, big dog."

A second later, the Riley kid takes off, and we follow him. Christmas music fills the air as the bands start to play. It pulsates my ears, as the drummer is right behind me. Bradley reaches down by his feet and pulls out a huge bag of candy. He hands it to Lacie.

She starts tossing candy, and both of them wave at everyone. "Wave, Collins." I do as Bradley says, then quickly regret it as I almost fall off the fender. Lacie snatches onto my arm and helps me adjust my seating. I smile down at her and scoot closer to her seat. Forget waving, nobody here knows me anyhow.

A few minutes later, we stop in front of the Piggly Wiggly. There are tons of people sitting in lawn chairs and truck beds all over the parking lot. It's like a modern-day conservative Woodstock or something.

Then Bradley puts the tractor brake on and we sit while the band begins to perform. The cheerleaders descend from a firetruck on down the parade line and come out front. The baton and flag girls join them and start dancing to "*Santa Claus is Coming to Town.*" An old man who looks like Kenny Rogers—before all the plastic surgery—gets out of a pickup and starts handing out candy. He's wearing a Santa suit and a cowboy hat.

The band gets louder, and the girls start getting more aggressive with their flags. I watch with caution until someone from the parking lot calls out, "Look, Lacie and Bradley are back together." Wait, what?

That's when I let my guard down and get smacked in the face by a flag pole. I lean back and tumble down the tractor and hit the ground. A collective gasp comes from the parking lot, and the music fizzles out.

Lacie is by my side in an instant. "Come help me!" she yells, and Bradley comes down. He hoists me over his shoulder like a duffle bag, which is impressive since we're relatively the same size. Not my best moment. Then he hauls me across the parking lot to the Piggly Wiggly. Lacie follows behind him. We walk through the automatic doors, and Bradley lays me across the grocery belt like I'm a sack of potatoes.

"Careful, Bradley," Lacie scolds him.

"Don't worry, Collins, I'm a paramedic."

Of course, he is. "And I'm a surgeon."

Bradley laughs. "Funny."

"He is a surgeon," Lacie snaps.

I muster a smile and raise to my elbows. "I just need to rest a minute. Nothing is broken, I assure you."

Lacie strokes my back and gives me a sympathetic face. "I'll take you home."

And let Bradley win? Never. "I'll be okay."

No sooner have those words left my mouth than the automatic doors open and an attractive blonde jogs past us best she can in heels and grabs some candy from a shelf. She slaps a twenty-dollar bill on the register beside me. "I forgot my snack." She clinches her teeth, then turns and walks out.

"Is that normal?" I ask.

"For her, yes," Bradley answers, as he cranes his head to watch her leave.

I shake my head and focus on sitting up. My leg will be sore tomorrow from hitting the pavement. But other than that, I should be fine. Lacie takes my arm and steadies me as I lift my legs off the belt and slide down to standing. She kisses my cheek and pats my back. "You're sure you don't want to go home?"

"I'm sure." In all honestly, there's nothing I'd rather do than throw in the towel and have Lacie drive me back to their house and nurse me back to health. But my inner caveman nature won't allow me to look weak in front of Bradley. Who, according to half the crowd, was once an item with Lacie.

"So, y'all feeling up to going to Mrs. Mary's?"

Lacie stares at me for an answer, even though I have no clue what Bradley is asking.

"Sure." Too late to back out now.

With Lacie latched onto my arm, we follow Bradley

outside. Someone has parked the tractor in the parking lot, and all the other vehicles are off the street as well. We walk a few blocks down the sidewalk and stop in front of a restaurant with "Diner" etched into a wooden sign.

Bradley opens the door to a room filled with people standing around eating and talking. Lacie leads me to the snack table and hands me a plate. She gently lets go of my arm and picks up a fancy cookie. "You've got to try these. My Aunt Carla made them." She piles a few on my plate. They're shaped and decorated like different Christmas ornaments. "Oh, and these are my mom's." She drops something chocolate beside the cookies.

"Excuse me." An older man in a bright striped shirt and a huge belt buckle breaks in front of us and puts some sweets in a Styrofoam box. Then he closes the lid and disappears.

We get a few more items and some hot chocolate. When we walk toward a row of booths, several people stare at me and whisper. No doubt I'm the talk of the town with my tractor tumble. I try extra hard not to limp and hide my pain as I crouch into the short booth.

Bradley is in the corner chatting up the pretty blonde. I catch Lacie eyeing him now and again, and I wish I had taken her up on that offer to go home.

CHAPTER FOUR

Lacie

I slide into the backseat of Daddy's truck and shut the door. Then I scoot closer to Collins and stare out at the Christmas lights as we pull out of the General Store parking lot. Collins reaches for my hand, and suddenly I'm fifteen again, in the back of my parents' car as they drive me and my boyfriend.

Awkward.

But not nearly as awkward as someone yelling, "Lacie and Bradley are back together," followed by Collins falling off the tractor.

"Collins, I hope you're feeling better." Mama smiles back at us.

"I am, thank you."

"You hit the ground pretty hard." Daddy laughs, until he catches my face in the rearview mirror.

"Yes, sir, I did." Collins raises an eyebrow at me.

"Good thing Bradley was there to pick you up," Daddy says.

Collins squeezes my hand, and I lean my head on his shoulder. I close my eyes and silently pray for Daddy to shut up. My prayer works, sort of. He doesn't shut up, but he changes the subject.

"I really thought Mary's would have more than sweets. Who's hungry?"

"I can make us some grilled cheese sandwiches when we get home," Mama says.

Daddy smiles at her, then shakes his head. "How about Wa-Ho?"

"Wa-Ho?" Collins turns to me in confusion.

"Daddy's pet name for Waffle House."

Collins nods.

"Is the Waffle House fine with everyone?" Mama looks back at us.

I try not to focus on Mama's need to put "the" in front of the restaurant name and instead channel my sarcasm elsewhere. "Well, that's kind of our only choice besides the gas station or Enchilada."

"Exactly." Daddy makes eye contact with me in the mirror.

We ride in silence the next few miles, then park in front of Waffle House. I'm surprised to find a decent-sized crowd this time of night, a few days before Christmas. Not so surprising is that they're all men wearing camouflage.

Daddy stops to talk to them. The rest of us greet them, then find a table near the back. A waitress who's about the size of an eleven-year-old comes over with menus and asks about drinks. Daddy rushes over and orders coffee, black. He's the only person I know who can drink coffee at ten p.m. and pass out as soon as his head hits the pillow.

Since I didn't inherit that trait, nor am I a fan of Wa-Ho

coffee, I order water. My vision blurs as I watch the lights change colors on the fiberoptic Christmas tree sitting above the grill.

The waitress comes back with our drinks and gets our food orders. She smiles for the first time, or at least that I notice, revealing a missing front tooth. I cut my eyes toward Collins, curious as to what he thinks about all this. He's leaned against the back of the booth, relaxed. I pat his knee under the table, and he takes my hand.

"Collin—"

"Collins, Daddy."

"Sorry, Collins." He overstresses the "s" and looks my way. I frown. "Would you believe this used to be Lacie Bug's favorite restaurant?"

Collins turns to me and lifts the corner of his mouth in a playful smirk. I shrug. "I like waffles."

A minute later, the waitress returns. This time, I notice a barbed wire tattooed across her weathered skin. I'm guessing there's a story behind that. She sets plates all around, and Daddy bows his head before she even walks away.

He voices a quick prayer, then immediately digs into his hash browns. Thankfully, what I did inherit from him was a good metabolism. Although, I haven't eaten a plate full of anything this late since undergrad. I wake up so early that it messes with my sleep.

Daddy takes a big gulp of coffee and sighs. Mama shakes her head. "I don't know how Joey drinks coffee this late."

"Or how he drinks this coffee, especially black," I add.

"Not every coffee has to cost ten bucks and come in an eco-friendly mermaid cup."

Collins's eyebrows squish together in confusion. I lean closer and whisper, "That's his way of making fun of my Star-bucks habit."

He lifts his chin and unfurrows his brow. Then he elbows

me under the table. He's always telling me I spend too much on coffee, too.

We start eating, with the ambiance of the deer hunters laughing behind us and dishes being slung in the sink at the grill. Typical late night in Wisteria.

Mama chatters about anything and everything to do with me growing up. Either G-Maw never embarrassed her like this, or she's forgotten how it feels. I muster through it until she mentions something about senior prom. Not that prom was bad, but she had to include that Bradley was my date.

As she continues, I chew my waffle and hope Collins overlooked that detail. He didn't.

"You went to prom with Bradley. Is that why people were saying you were back together?"

I choke on my waffle and scramble for my water like someone backpacking through the Sahara beneath the midday sun. The cold liquid dislodges the syrupy mush caught in my throat, but still makes me cough.

Before I can steer the conversation elsewhere, Daddy steps in. Or more like steps on his tongue. "Nah, I think they said that because we all thought they'd get married."

Now, I'm coughing so loudly that I can't catch my breath. Mama's eyes widen with concern. I finally manage to catch a breath when she hits Daddy in the chest.

"Ouch. What was that for?"

Seriously? He's so clueless. I glance at Collins, who's calmly picking apart his omelet. "We were never gonna get married. All Daddy means is that we dated for several years, and most people in a small town who date someone from their same town for an extended period of time usually marry that person. That's all."

Mama offers me a clinched-jaw smile and pitying eyes. I don't know whether that means she's sorry I'm in this situation or she thinks I'm a fool for believing Bradley and I weren't on the marriage track.

"It doesn't matter. I broke up with him years back, and then last year, I met Collins." I smile at him and squeeze his knee under the table. He flinches and grits his teeth, then halfway smiles at me. I forgot that leg took a heavy hit an hour earlier. "Can we please talk about something else? Anything else. Christmas, hunting, deworming cattle, how our ninety-pound waitress ended up with a biker tattoo on her bicep?"

Either words carry in Waffle House or I was louder than intended, because our waitress looks up from the cash register and answers, "It's from my ex. He didn't do rings, so we got matching marriage tattoos before going to Vegas."

"Thank you," I mutter toward her, then drop my head to hide the heat rising in my cheeks.

Collins grabs my hand under the table, probably out of pity by this point. "Okay, so I have a question."

"Shoot." Daddy talks around a mouthful of bacon.

"All these Wisteria people were in the Apple Cart parade, and Apple Cart seems to have all of the shopping."

"Except for the Dollar General," Mama adds. The place she can't go more than three days without visiting.

Collins nods and half smiles at Mama before continuing. "So, they have different names, but aren't they really like the same place?"

I guess words do carry in Waffle House, because Collins wasn't loud at all. Yet every hunter at the bar quits talking immediately. It's so awkwardly quiet, you could hear a mouse peeing on cotton, as G-Maw would say.

We all stare at each other a second before Daddy yells, "Check, please!"

Collins

I DON'T KNOW what I said in Waffle House, but it made a dozen men with guns stare me down as intently as Bradley stared down the ditsy blonde leaving Piggly Wiggly.

Bradley. I puff up my cheeks and let out a breath.

"You okay?" Lacie rubs my arm. I look back at her. "Yeah." I feign a smile, then lay my head back against the headrest.

The truth is, I'm not okay. I haven't managed to make a good impression on her dad, and with every minute, I'm further away from asking him if I can marry his daughter. For one thing, he intimidates me. For another, he lights up whenever Bradley is around. And he said himself that everyone thought Bradley and Lacie would get married.

I had nothing against the dude until I found out he was Lacie's first and only long-term relationship besides me. After that epiphany, I realize why he laughed at me saying I was with Lacie.

I grind my teeth to keep from screaming. I've pulled all-nighters, scrubbing in on multiple emergency surgeries, and this is still the longest night of my life.

Finally, we pull up to their house. I get out slowly, so as not to aggravate my sore leg. Lacie's mom folds her arms and rushes to the front door. There's a chill in the air, and I'm glad it's not just me. All I need now is to pass out from my fall.

Lacie and I walk up the porch at a leisurely pace. She pulls her jacket on and sits in a rocking chair. I sit in the one beside her. "It's gotten a lot colder since the ride home," I say.

"I told you. That cold front is here."

I laugh. "You still predicting a white Christmas?"

Lacie's face tightens. "Absolutely. I wouldn't be surprised if Jim Vann called it anytime now."

I laugh harder. She's shared with me why she wanted to work in weather, including her obsession with Jim Vann the Weather Man. It's one of the adorable things I love most about her.

"Hey, I'm so sorry about tonight." Her face drops, and she reaches for my hand.

"Which part?" I grin, and she laughs.

"Bradley's like some sort of hero around here. He was a star quarterback in high school, and now he's the county sheriff. Daddy has never seen me with anyone else, and he's protective. He doesn't know you yet."

"That's exactly why I wanted to spend Christmas here." Well, and I plan to propose. But now is definitely not the time for that. "I wish you'd brought me here sooner. I've wondered if you were embarrassed of me or something."

Lacie's jaw drops. "No, no, no, not at all! I'm embarrassed of my life."

I scrunch my forehead. "Your life? You have a great life."

"Yeah, have, not had. Growing up in a place like Wisteria, with a bunch of gun-crazed relatives who kill and eat hogs on Christmas."

"You never told me you kill your own hogs."

"See, and that's why. I wish you could see your face right now. But we don't kill *our* hogs. We'd never kill a pet."

I try my best to neutralize my expression. But in my defense, it's not every day I hear about people making their own bacon in modern-day America.

"My daddy is enough of an embarrassment, and you haven't even met the rest of the family."

"So. What's so bad about your family?"

Lacie drops her head in her hands and groans. "My uncle

lives and breathes guns. And his son just got out of jail for stealing mail."

I blink, partly in shock at the jail statement and partly in shock at someone stealing mail. "Like packages or checks?"

Lacie shakes her head. "Netflix DVDs and Victoria Secret's catalogues."

"Wow."

She lifts her eyes at me. "I know." She sits back in her chair and rocks slowly. "My aunt has been married more times than I know about and has six kids ranging in age from thirty to a baby. She's obsessed with Dolly Parton and wears clothes nobody her age should even consider trying on."

"Well, you can't help any of that."

Lacie lifts the corner of her lips into a crooked smile, then frowns again. "I know. I guess I just thought I'd wait until we were married before subjecting you to such a circus."

I put my other hand on top of hers and rub it with my thumb. My heart pounds against my chest at her mention of marrying me. Especially after all the Bradley crap tonight. It takes everything in me to not drop to one knee right here and propose. Instead, I pull her closer to me and run my thumb over her cheek.

"Lacie, I love you, and nobody or nothing could change my mind."

She leans in and kisses me. I wrap my arms around her shoulders and melt into her embrace. For the first time since I arrived in Wisteria, something feels normal. The longer we kiss, the more confidence I gain in resuming my proposal plan.

Then the porch light blinks fast enough to give me a seizure. Lacie pulls back and sighs. She stands and pulls me up with her. "Time to go in."

We walk in the living room, where her mom is sitting on

the couch watching TV. "I didn't want you kids to stay out too long and get cold."

Lacie frowns at me, then turns to her mom. "Sure you didn't."

Mrs. Sanderson smiles at me. "I stocked the basement fridge for you. Lacie can show you where everything is." Then she turns to Lacie. "Just don't stay down there longer than necessary, honey."

"I won't." Lacie's face is flat as she passes her mom and leads me downstairs. On the way down, she whispers, "One more annoyance I forgot to include."

"It's fine, really." I give her a reassuring grin. She shakes her head and continues toward the basement.

"Okay, here's the refrigerator. I told her you like Mountain Dew, so there's that and some water and Gatorades. And here are the snacks." She opens a cabinet above the refrigerator to show me nuts and chips.

"Thanks."

"The bathroom is right there." She points to the door. "And it looks like Mama has made the bed." She nods in the opposite direction toward a mattress on the floor that is now made up with the sheets Mrs. Sanderson brought down during one of her earlier interruptions.

Lacie walks over to me and wraps her arms around my neck. "Now, I best get upstairs before my curfew." Her eyes dance as she laughs.

"Yes, ma'am." I kiss her gently on the lips, then release her to go upstairs. "Love you."

She stops at the base of the stairs and smiles at me. "Love you, too."

I watch until her feet disappear and I hear the door to the basement shut. Then I go brush my teeth and change into my pajamas. I haven't slept on a mattress on the floor since college. And even then it wasn't intentional. But I could sleep on the roof tonight, as tired as I am.

A few minutes later, I crawl into bed—more like onto mattress—and reach up to switch off the lamp on the desk beside me. As I situate the pillow beneath my head, my eyes land on the opposite wall. Numerous animal heads are mounted across from me. Mostly deer like upstairs, but one larger head in the center disturbs me. It's the largest boar or hog, or whatever, I've ever seen. Its mouth is open, with huge teeth and a tongue hanging out. Even worse, the moonlight coming in from the small window beside it casts shadows resembling war paint across its face.

I turn on my side and grab the second pillow, covering my face. But I can't shake the image from my mind. Especially knowing it's right across the wall from me. What if that thing falls off in the middle of the night and rolls toward me? It's got to weight several hundred pounds. I shudder and pull my legs in closer to my waist.

What is wrong with me? A twenty-seven-year-old man living in downtown Atlanta shouldn't be scared of a dead pig head. But I am. Or at least intimidated by it. In Atlanta, all we have to worry about are wrecks and shootings and armed robberies. There's no chance of me waking up to a giant, hairy pig face ready to gobble me up.

All I can say is that Lacie better know I love her. More than anything.

CHAPTER FIVE

Lacie

When you're expected to be perky on camera before the sun comes up, sleeping until seven a.m. is a luxury. I climb out of bed and stretch, then roll my eyes at the photos on the opposite wall of my room. I can't believe Mama hasn't redecorated it by now. I told her when I went to college she could use my room however she wanted. I think she secretly thought I'd move back to Alabama after school, or perhaps visit overnight more often.

But an adult room might entice me to stay more than a different color paint on each wall, half covered by photos from high school.

The sun is peeking through my curtains. I pull one back and smile at the scattered clouds coming in. Still, nobody believes me about the snow. Fine by me. They'll be sorry when we're all on an apocalyptic mission to the Pig for bread and milk.

Since my body won't allow me to sleep any longer, I change into running clothes and pull my hair back into a ponytail. As I'm in the bathroom brushing my teeth, I hear a blood-curling scream from below.

Then I remember Collins. Not that I forgot him, but I forgot that he's here . . . in the basement.

I spit out my toothpaste, rinse the sink, and jog downstairs. There's my brother, wearing nothing more than a pair of gym shorts and holding a huge knife while standing over Collins.

"Liam, what are you doing?"

"I'm gettin' my blade to sharpen for the hog killin'. Why is he in the basement?"

"Because he's spending Christmas here."

"I thought he left."

I roll my eyes and walk closer to the crime scene. "No, why would you think that?"

Liam snickers. "If I fell off a tractor in front of the whole county, I think I'd leave. No, I know I'd leave."

I slap my forehead. "Please, just leave us alone."

Liam backs up a few feet and raises his hands. "Fine."

Collins gets out of bed. Liam laughs. "Nice PJs."

Collins is wearing the plaid pajamas I bought him for his birthday. I know he doesn't get to sleep often, and when he does, he likes to be comfortable. "Liam, not everyone sleeps in shorts."

"Hey, me neither. I put these on before coming down here out of respect for you guys."

I sigh. Dear Lord, give me strength.

"Sorry, sis." Liam taps my shoulder with his free hand and lowers the knife. "I'm gonna go sharpen my blade. We're gonna pick up the hog after breakfast."

"You do that." I shake my head and sigh.

Liam slugs upstairs, laughing when his head is out of

sight. He's too dense to know we can still hear him . . . and see his legs.

Collins yawns. "Where do they get the hog?"

"Our friend Jack usually hooks them up. We got one from a farm in Wisteria once, but it tasted bad."

Collins's eyes widen. "Where's this Jack guy?"

"Apple Cart. He raises deer and turkey, but knows some other hunting camps that raise hogs."

"Hunting camps?"

"Yeah, like where you go and pay to kill stuff."

"Huh?"

I take for granted that everyone eats, sleeps, and breathes hunting like my dad and brother.

"So they buy a hog, then y'all kill it, then eat it?"

I waver my head. "Sometimes Jack donates the hog so that he can get some of the meat."

"Wow."

I laugh. "It's not as barbaric as it sounds. I promise, this is some of the best bacon you'll ever taste."

Collins lifts his chin and raises his eyebrows. I don't think he's fully convinced we're not serial killers. Not that waking up to Liam wielding a knife over him would help debunk that hypothesis.

"What do you do with the head? Mount it like that?" He raises his eyes, and I follow his gaze to the boar's head behind me.

"Nah. That one is special. Daddy killed it on a big hunt. We boil our hog heads."

"Why?"

"You can use the broth in soup, or my G-Maw sometimes uses the fatty meat to make jelly."

Collins's face grows pale and he rushes past me toward the bathroom. He swings open the door and hugs the toilet.

I wince and turn my head as he spills his guts. I guess I've said too much.

I want to check on him, but also want to give him some space, so I stand back and wait for him to come out. He flushes the toilet and gurgles some mouthwash before sliding back into the main room.

"You okay?"

He shrugs. "I think I just need more sleep."

I nod. "I was gonna run, but I can stay here if you want."

He lifts a palm and shakes his head. "Go, I'll sleep."

I nod and give him a closed-lipped smile. I tiptoe upstairs as he collapses onto the mattress and pulls the covers over his head. Then I sneak out of the house before anyone asks anything else of me. With all the stress of last night, I could use a good run to clear my head.

The air is crisp with a slight breeze. I breath in the fresh scent of pine as I start down our driveway. When I get to G-Paw and G-Maw's house, Woody is peeing off the front steps of his RV. When he sees me, he turns around, peeing on his door in the process.

I bite back a laugh and jog onto the main road. Unlike Atlanta, there aren't any neighborhood streets to run on. But also unlike Atlanta, there isn't any traffic on the main roads.

I run a good mile or two, staring up at the sky now and again. The clouds are moving in, just like I predicted. Only two days before Christmas, and all is shaping into place for snow. And not just a dusting. Actual snow. We're talking blizzard of '93 snow, which I wasn't fortunate enough to see in real life.

I poke out my bottom lip at missing such a momentous snow. If I'd only been born a few years sooner. A police siren blares behind me, giving me one more reason to wish I'd been born sooner.

I wouldn't have had romantic history with Bradley Manning.

I roll my eyes and slow to a walk. Might as well get this over with. That is so Bradley, to use his authority to his advantage. I wonder how many women he pulls over on a daily basis.

He pulls up beside me and rolls down the window. "Get in."

I squint, hoping he can catch the death glare in my eyes through his too-dark *Top Gun* glasses. Then I turn my head and speed to a jog. He speeds up to match my pace.

"Get in, Lacie."

"No."

"Yes."

"Why?"

"I want to talk to you."

"Well, I have nothing to say to you."

"Please, just a minute."

I stop, and so does he. I cross my arms and take a few deep breaths. Both from running and from running into him. "Will you leave me alone after this?"

"Yes."

I halfway don't believe him, but it's worth a shot. Plus, I'm getting a little tired since I'm used to running on concrete rather than asphalt. Against my better judgement, I open the door and hop in. After I shut the door, he rolls up my window. I recross my arms and stare through the windshield.

"I want to apologize for last night."

"Oh, you do? For asking me to sit on your lap, for slamming Collins down on a Piggly Wiggly conveyer belt, or for just being yourself in general?"

"For everything."

I blink at his answer. Part of me wants to ask if this includes beyond last night, but my goal is to get out of this cop car ASAP, not start World War III.

Bradley dips his head and removes his glasses. I study his face for the first time since I've come home. He's still hand-some—dark features, chiseled jaw, and all. But he's got a few crinkles in the crease of his eyes now, and nothing about his face sends flutters through my stomach like it did before.

In high school and throughout most of my college years, staring into his dark eyes would make me swoon. He used to say we'd have the most beautiful dark-eyed, dark-haired babies one day. I'd eat it up like ice cream. That is, until one day that comment gave me a different kind of flutter. It made me nauseated.

For most of our college days, we'd take turns visiting one another on weekends. And sometimes he'd even surprise me at State during the week, as it was only an hour's drive from Tuscaloosa. And every few weeks, I noticed a change. Not in him, but me.

College made me grow up. I no longer cared so much about having a booming social life or clothes and makeup. I chose studying over parties and matured my look to fewer crop tops and more camera-worthy attire. I wanted to do all I could to ensure I'd get a job at The Weather Channel.

Bradley, on the other hand, was a slightly older version of himself. If not worse. No longer an athlete, he immersed himself in everything Alabama football, as if vicariously living through others. He barely skated through classes to keep his parents satisfied. He partied—a lot—and all he talked about was moving back home to join the police force. I couldn't see him in Atlanta, and I couldn't see me not in Atlanta.

So one night, as we sat on my couch sharing pizza and

popcorn, I broke up with him. At first, he thought I was joking. Then he tried to talk me out of it. When I asked him to leave, he got mad. He said we were meant to be together and that I'd regret that decision the rest of my life.

Four years later, and I still don't regret it.

He tilts his head, and I lean back against the window. If he tries to make a move on me, I'll punch him, then bail.

Instead, he glares out the windshield and chews on the stem of his glasses. "Why Collins?"

"Excuse me?"

He faces me again, glasses hanging from his bottom lip. Surely he doesn't think this look is seductive, because it's disgusting.

"You could have anyone in the world, but you chose him."

I shake my head and laugh. Not a "haha, that's funny" kind of laugh. More like the kind of laugh that comes from a mixture of sleep deprivation and hysteria. "Collins is a wonderful, intelligent, caring man. He's a freakin' surgeon, for crying out loud. And not that it matters as much, but he's handsome, too." I rake my hand through my ponytail and sigh.

Bradley shrugs and tosses his glasses on the dash. "If you say so."

I bite my bottom lip and blow steam out my nostrils. "Bradley, the only problem you have with Collins is that he's not you. And that's precisely what I love about him."

Not taking the time to punch Bradley in the face, I open the car door and run in the opposite direction.

Collins

I ROLL over and rub my eyes. I have no idea what time it is and momentarily wonder where I am. Then I notice a gun in the corner and a mounted fox by the refrigerator. Right, I'm in the wax museum of stuffed road kill, aka Lacie's family's basement.

Most people have like a game console or a pool table in their basement. Or at least a treadmill and some boxes. Nope, this family collects dead animals.

I sit up, stretch, and check my Apple Watch on the desk next to my bed, uh, mattress. Eight-thirty. I get out of bed and change, then I brush my teeth and try not to think about vomiting earlier. My stomach growls when I swallow some water. Maybe there's something to eat upstairs besides pig brains. I shudder at the image that conjures up.

Mrs. Sanderson and Lacie's candy looked good. Maybe Liam hasn't eaten it all. I typically steer clear of sweets in the morning, but nothing about this trip has been typical.

I slip on my shoes and head upstairs, where I smell cinnamon rolls. Perfect. Everyone is sitting around the table in the kitchen. I pull out the chair beside Lacie and sit down.

"Collins, help yourself. Sorry we started without you. Lacie said to let you sleep."

"Thank you, Mrs. Sanderson," I say, reaching for a plate and putting a cinnamon roll on it. Then I scoop a spoonful of eggs, but pause when I come to the bacon. I can't get pig brains out of my head. I may never eat pork again.

Lacie watches me hesitate over the bacon, then gives me a mischievous smile. She knows how much I love bacon and has obviously read my mind. I smile back at her.

Mr. Sanderson is reading what appears to be a local paper. I haven't seen anyone read a printed newspaper in years. But they have no cell phone service, so I guess an online subscription isn't an option. And Liam still isn't wearing a shirt.

I stare down at my plate to avoid the peach fuzz on Liam's chest across the table from me. Nobody seems to care, or even notice, that the guy isn't wearing a shirt at the breakfast table. Except me. I refocus my mind on the yoga pants Lacie is wearing instead. With a much more attractive picture now in my head, I bite off a piece of my cinnamon roll. Man, that's good. My hungry stomach churns when the food hits it.

"What are your plans for today, Lacie?" Mrs. Sanderson asks.

Lacie shrugs at her mom, then turns to me. "I was thinking maybe we could go into Tuscaloosa later for lunch. There's a great local sushi place. Then maybe we could ice skate and grab coffee."

"Ha." Mr. Sanderson folds his paper and stares at Lacie. "You kids and sushi. There's raw fish out back in the pond." He waves a hand toward the window.

"Joey." Mrs. Sanderson frowns at him.

"What?" Mr. Sanderson shrugs.

Lacie doesn't say a word, and Liam is in his own world eating his third cinnamon roll. That is, since I've been here. Maybe he's eaten even more. I don't get how this kid is so skinny. Maybe sharpening knives burns more calories than you'd think.

"If you want to go ice skating, you should just go up to the school," Mrs. Sanderson suggests.

"The school?" Lacie puts down her fork and frowns at her mother. "What school?"

"Your school, Wisteria High."

Lacie laughs so hard that she coughs and has to get a drink of her coffee.

"Mama, she doesn't know, because she never comes home." Liam speaks up for the first time in between cinnamon rolls.

Lacie leans over the table. "That's not true." Then she turns to her mom. "At least not the 'never comes home' part. I honestly don't know what you're talking about."

"The Women's Club in town helped convert the practice field into a skating rink. Thanks to the cooler weather and a bunch of box fans, we were able to freeze some of the field."

"And you think we should skate there instead of Tuscaloosa?" Lacie continues to stare at her mom.

"Well, just a thought. It's so much closer, and that way Collins can see where you went to school."

I want to say I'd like to see her old school, but Lacie's face communicates hesitation. She and Mrs. Sanderson both stare at me for an answer. Even checked-out Liam looks my way, and Mr. Sanderson glances up from his paper.

"I'll do whatever Lacie wants."

"Smart man." Mr. Sanderson meets my gaze with an expressionless face. He's not laughing at me, so I'll take that as a compliment. Small victories.

"You should take him, Lacie," Liam mumbles with a mouthful of food. "Some of us went the other night. They have real skates and everything."

Lacie exhales and leans back in her chair. "Real skates? As opposed to, what, wearing rubber boots like we do when the pond freezes over?"

Liam nods. "Yeah." His face is stone-cold serious. Poor kid. Then again, he does attend Auburn.

Lacie tugs at the end of her ponytail, which she only does when she's nervous. I look back at my plate. Everyone else is putting enough pressure on her as it is. After an eternal moment of silence, she answers, "Fine. We'll check it out. But if Collins doesn't like it, we're heading for T-town."

Mr. Sanderson and Liam laugh and smile, while Mrs. Sanderson claps and cheers as if Lacie just agreed to something life-changing. Like maybe marrying me. I can only hope this family would get excited over that.

CHAPTER SIX

Lacie

Against my better judgment, I park in front of my alma mater. Not Mississippi State—the one before that. The parking lot is still full of potholes, so I try and dodge those accordingly. I turn off the engine and hop out. Collins follows.

"Well, here we are. Good ole Wisteria High School." I fan my hands around Vanna White style to match my sarcastic tone.

"Nothing wrong with this. It's typical brick and metal buildings."

I smile, glad I have someone in my life who always sees the upside of things. We walk across the parking lot, careful to not roll an ankle as we navigate the potholes. I immediately see a group of women from high school. They weren't the nicest to me, but I put on a pleasant face. At least, I think it's pleasant.

"Hey, Lacie. How's life as a celebrity?"

I grit my teeth. "I wouldn't know."

Candy—yes, that's her birth name—swats at my arm. "Oh now, don't be so modest. You're on cable TV."

I nod, but say nothing. I'm informing the world about weather patterns, not exactly shaking my tail feathers on *Dancing with the Stars*. Not that any of those people are actual celebrities, in my opinion.

"Is this your husband?" Trista asks, while eyeing Collins like he's the seventy-five-percent-off rack at Belk.

"My boyfriend," I correct her. My clarification only makes her inch closer to him. "You're married, right?"

She shakes her head. "Not anymore."

"Well, it's been nice talking to you ladies, we're going to head this way." I jerk Collins's arm and continue toward the fields with the gusto of an Olympic speed walker. My desire to escape the mean girls now outweighs my caution for tripping in the parking lot.

We miraculously make it to the fields unscathed. I nod and offer a "hey" to many people we pass, but cling to Collins to try and give off a vibe that says, "I'm not being unfriendly, I'm just preoccupied." Maybe people buy it. Truth be told, I'm more worried about someone bringing up the Bradley saga or something else embarrassing from my past. Running into Regina George and her number-one goon a minute ago was enough for one visit home. This is precisely why I tend to limit my Christmas outings to G-Maw's house and church.

We stop in front of the walkway between the practice field and the game field. Oddly enough, there's also a cattle field that runs behind both. It's owned by one of the larger farms in town. They donated some land to the school years ago, so nobody has the guts to ask them to move their cows.

Even though we've had several instances of loose cattle at the most inconvenient times . . . like the state playoff game.

I start toward the practice field, the hum of box fans roaring as we get closer. Collins slows down and asks, "Why is there a cow on your football field?"

I don't bother to turn my attention toward the bigger field. "It probably got out from the farm that backs up to the school. It happens more than you'd think."

"Oh. Do you guys play other sports on this field?"

I shake my head. "Just football."

Collins stops altogether, causing me to stop, too, since I still have a death grip on his bicep. "Strange. I've never seen markings like that on a field. I thought maybe it was for some kind of other sport I don't know about."

My body begins to numb. I close my eyes and voice a silent prayer. *Dear God, don't let it be.* I finally muster up the courage to turn my head and discover that my worst nightmare has come true. Well, aside from the one I lived out yesterday with Bradley.

Sure enough, there's a cow meandering around the field. Red squares are painted all across the grass, with a number inside each. This isn't some kind of obscure sport or even a mass cake walk. Nope. It's the dang cow-patty drop. But why are they doing it at Christmastime?

"Lacie?" I shift my eyes to find Kyle Tolbert, yet another person from high school . . . who happens to be Bradley's best friend.

"Hi, Kyle."

He side hugs me, which is a little awkward since I'm still holding onto Collins. "How have you been? I haven't seen you in years."

"Good." I motion toward Collins with my free hand. "This is Collins."

"Hey, nice to meet you, Kyle Tolbert." He extends his hand, and Collins shakes it.

"Collins O'Conner, nice to meet you as well."

Kyle steps back and glances down at the clipboard he's holding, then back at us. "So, what made you decide to come back after all these years?"

I grit my teeth, trying not to take it personally. I come back every year, sometimes more than that. I just keep to my family road. Instead of arguing my point, I simply respond, "Mama suggested we check out the skating rink while we're in town. But I see y'all are doing the cow-patty drop . . . at Christmas?" My proclamation ends like a question as I refocus my attention on the cow swishing its tail.

"Oh yeah. It's a fundraiser for the Angel Tree."

"Okay, well that's a good idea. Does the winner still get some prize money?"

"Yeah, same as we do pre-football season."

I nod. Collins wrinkles his brow and turns to me, then Kyle. "How does this game work, exactly?"

"People purchase a square. If the cow poops on their square, they win. Simple as that." Kyle leans toward us and holds up the clipboard. One page has a graphed model of the field, complete with numbers in all the squares. The next page has a list of all those numbers with a name by each one.

"That's a lot of names," Collins comments.

Kyle nods. "We sold out every single square in record time."

Collins squints and tilts his head toward the list of names. "What's an Apple Cart County Tractor Pull Association?"

Kyle grins. "Oh, that's the tractor pull club. If we win, we'll use the money to put toward a sled upgrade."

"Like a Santa sled?"

I stare at my boots. I'm embarrassed for Collins at this

point. Thank God, Kyle is so nice and not one to tease. Unlike his bestie, Bradley.

"It's what we call the piece of equipment the tractors pull in the competition."

"Oh, sounds neat."

Kyle nods. "It really is. You should talk Lacie into bringing you back this summer to see it."

I look back at Collins, who is all smiles. A small part of me melts at how he's taking all of this in without an ounce of sarcasm or making fun of our oddball extracurriculars.

Before Kyle can say anything else, a loud bellow comes from the field. Tall as he is, he still cranes his head for a better view. "Oh, Petunia's raising her tail. I think this contest is about to end. You guys enjoy yourselves."

"Thanks, nice seeing you, Kyle."

He waves a hand in the air as he jogs down to the field. Before he makes it down, people passing by start cheering. The cow has pooped.

"Well, that was interesting." Collins takes a step toward the field and watches.

This might be fascinating to him, but I've seen my fair share of cow poop in my life. "Ready to skate?"

"Sure." He smiles as I pull him toward the roar of box fans and away from the pooping cow.

We stop at the entrance to the rink, where a slouchy woman with pink hair and a nose ring sits behind a table. Not a stud nose ring, but a hoop that's latched to both nostrils. I'm not sure how she got it in there or how it cooperates with sneezing. But I'm happy to say she is not from my high school. At least not in the time I was here.

"Two tickets?"

"Yes, please." Collins pulls out his wallet and hands her his check card.

She drops her jaw and pokes her bottom lip out like a trout taking the bait. "Uh, we don't take cards."

"It's debit."

"Doesn't matter. Not enough service here to run it through."

Collins rubs his beard and sighs. The man never carries cash.

"I got it." I open my small crossbody bag and pull out a folded twenty-dollar bill.

"Perfect." She takes my money and hands me four dollars in change. Then she points a long, black fingernail behind her head. "Skates are back that way at the booth."

"Thank you." Collins smiles at her, but she's already looking down at her phone.

We walk behind her to the skate stand and give the older man inside our sizes. He brings me a pair of sevens. I get a little giddy when I see that they're brown with red laces. Just like in one of my Christmas movies. Most of the skates in Atlanta resemble rollerblades.

"Just a minute." He clicks his teeth, then turns back to rummage through the shelves. He comes back with two mismatched skates. "This here's all we got in a men's eleven. I'm afraid some of those teenagers didn't return all their skates."

Collins holds the skates up and examines the bottoms, as if making sure they will stand the same. The man removes his CO-OP cap and scratches his head. "Sorry, son. If you want to wait and see if one comes in . . ."

"No, sir, I'm sure I can manage." Collins sets the skates upright and smiles. "Thank you."

"Okay." The man replaces his cap and presses his thin lips together. We walk over to a row of hay bales where other people are sitting, changing out their shoes and skates.

I put on my Hallmark skates and watch as poor Collins

slips on a red skate and a black one. The black one is way bulkier and taller once he stands up. But he's a good sport about it and hobbles toward the rink with me.

We climb onto the ice, my scarf whipping my face as we pass the row of box fans. I'm both surprised and thankful that it's frozen solid. Collins comes right behind me, one knee a little bent to compensate for the uneven skates.

He grips my hand and does his best to skate by my side. He's such a good skater back home in matching skates. Now, he's hobbled over and clinging to my arm. I can't help but laugh, which makes Collins laugh, too.

We inch around the rink a little farther before he bends forward, chuckling, pulling us both to the ground in the process. We lie there and laugh, not caring that people are passing us. Collins pulls me toward him and kisses me.

And in that moment, I don't care about the lack of ambiance in the air—fans can blow and cows can poop. Who cares? I'm in love.

Collins

THE ONLY THING worse than falling from a tractor and hitting your leg on asphalt is having to then bend that leg to try and skate on uneven skates the next day.

Lacie and I didn't even make it around the rink before we were a pile of mush on the ice. But Lacie was a good sport about it, laughing on the way down. She makes everything more fun. Before having her in my life, I was stressed and lonely, living a mundane routine of work, TV and eating at sports bars with my roommates. She's good for me.

I pull some slack on my seat belt and shift in my seat to take the pressure off my throbbing leg. I walked away from that frozen ground like a champ, but I'm paying for it now. As we pull up to the Sandersons' house, all I can think about is propping my leg up for a while.

Once we get within a few feet of the garage, Lacie's dad holds up his hand for us to stop. Then Liam drives in front of us and parks in front of the garage. A huge hog sticks its snout over the side of the truck bed.

"Looks like they're back with the hog." Lacie says this nonchalantly, as if it's part of everyday life. But I guess it is for them.

I get out and shut my door, then follow her to the truck. By now, Mrs. Sanderson is outside standing beside us. Mr. Sanderson climbs up into the bed of the truck and holds onto the pig. Liam opens the tailgate and joins him.

Mrs. Sanderson crosses her arms and steps toward the truck. "Why did you bring it here?"

Mr. Sanderson turns his gaze from the pig to his wife. "Your mom's goats ate through their fence again, and I'm not putting up with Earl and Carla complaining that the hog pooped on their high-dollar grass."

Mrs. Sanderson frowns. "So where are you gonna put it?"

"In the dog pen," he answers through gritted teeth as he shoves the heavy hog toward the edge of the truck.

Curious as to how they'll get that thing out, I crane my neck for a better view. Then Liam slides a large board of plywood down from the bed, angling it like a ramp. He holds the board with one hand and helps pull the pig with the other.

For a split second, I think about offering to help. But my leg is still throbbing from the two falls, and I'm not sure how I would help.

Liam pulls the beast down the plywood, only to have it

break through halfway down. The hog lands on its back and grunts. Mrs. Sanderson brings her hands to her mouth and gasps. Her eyes grow as big as quarters.

Lacie's shoulders shake as she fights off a laugh. I stand there in awe as thin-as-a-rail Liam manages to flip the pig back on its feet. Then he loops his arm around its neck and guides it to a nearby pen. Mr. Sanderson hops down from the truck and follows.

The pig's belly drags the ground as they stumble toward their destination. I can only imagine how much this thing weighs. Its head alone is huge. I hold my mouth and swallow down a bit of vomit at the thought of boiling it.

Once they get the pig inside the pen, a huge dog I haven't noticed until now emerges from a dog house. He shows his teeth and growls.

"Bully, calm down, baby." Mrs. Sanderson walks toward the pen and speaks as if he were a kitten rather than a massive bullmastiff. I don't know what they feed animals around here, but it's working.

Bully doesn't listen. Instead, he darts at the pig and tries to bite. The pig is surprisingly agile and dodges the bite. Mr. Sanderson grabs the dog's collar and drags it out of the pen. "Bully, you're gonna stay inside until Myrtle is meat."

I widen my eyes. I can't believe they named a pig they plan on eating. Then again, none of this is normal to me.

"Why can't he just stay in the yard?" Mrs. Sanderson wrinkles her nose at Bully. Funny how quickly she went from calling him baby to not wanting him around.

"No, Robin. The mutt down the road is in heat. Again." Mr. Sanderson's words clip each time Bully moves. He somehow manages to keep the dog from breaking free, despite Bully sniffing the air like a drug dog. He must pick up the mutt's pheromones. Or perhaps that dead skunk off the main road.

"But he'll drink all my tree water."

"Then we'll keep him in the basement with the artificial tree."

Now it's my turn to wrinkle my nose. The last thing I want is to share a space with a dog that outweighs Lacie. If I weren't trying to prove myself to Mr. Sanderson, I might just offer to find a hotel.

Liam leaves the pen and closes Myrtle inside. She—I'm assuming by the name—rolls over in the corner and snorts. He comes over to Bully and takes his collar. "I've got 'em, Daddy."

Mr. Sanderson lets go of Bully, only to have him dart off toward the driveway, jerking Liam down in the process. Mr. Sanderson runs full speed and tackles the bullmastiff to the ground. I'm both impressed and terrified. Then he snatches his collar and leads him in the direction of the basement. They disappear behind the house.

With the show over, the rest of us go inside through the front door. I catch a whiff of Liam as he passes me in the doorway. He smells like a literal pigsty.

Between my sore leg and Liam's smell, I make the easy decision to retreat to my room. "I'm going to go lie down for a bit, if that's okay."

"Yeah. I'll come make sure Bully's out of your way." Lacie smiles and follows me toward the basement stairs.

Right . . . I momentarily forget there's a canine room-mate waiting for me.

We reach the bottom of the stairs to find the dog rolling on his back in the middle of my mattress. Great. Just great.

Out of instinct, I reach for his collar to pull him down. He growls and bites at my hand. I snatch it back, and Lacie takes charge.

"Bully, get down!"

He flips over and leaps off the mattress at Lacie's command. Impressive.

"Thanks?" I'm still in awe of how well he minds her.

"Good boy." She pets his head, which comes up to her chest. Then she grabs hold of his collar and leads him to the corner of the room. She pulls a throw from off the couch and folds it on the floor. "Sit." He sits on the blanket. "Now you can go ahead and rest," she says to me.

I walk to the mattress and plop down. Lacie sits beside me and leans her head on my shoulder, and I wrap her in a hug. She raises her head to meet my face, and we start kissing. About a minute into our kiss, I hear growling behind me. I pull back to see Bully, back on the bed, staring at me.

"Bully, it's okay. We like Collins." She pets him, and he calms a bit. But he continues growling lowly.

Lacie continues petting him and turns to me. "He just needs to get used to you. He's very protective of our family."

"I can see that." I inch closer to the edge of the mattress. Lacie scoots closer to me and kisses me again.

I think I hear footsteps, but I'm not sure with the growling behind my head. I try to ignore both and just focus on Lacie.

"Lacie!"

She pulls back this time and flinches at her dad's stern voice.

"Daddy, I'm twenty-five."

"But you're under my roof."

"We weren't doing anything."

"You're on a bed."

Technically, sir, we're on a mattress, as you didn't give me a bed. I bite my tongue so that thought won't materialize into words.

"We're sitting up, fully dressed in winter coats, just kissing."

"Doesn't matter." Mr. Sanderson jerks his head, and Lacie hops up as if she's a puppet and he's pulled her string.

I sit petrified. Do I get up, too, or stay here? Bully has stopped growling at me. I guess since Lacie got up. But he's now rolling on his back again. Then, to top off the awkwardness, Liam slips out from inside the closet with two guns. I didn't even know he was down here.

Mr. Sanderson turns from Lacie to Liam. "No, put that one back. Get the other one."

Liam comes back with one of the same guns and another one. Mr. Sanderson nods in approval, then turns to me.

I wipe my clammy palms on my pants, waiting for a speech about dating his daughter. Instead, he shocks me with, "Collins, you need to come shoot with us."

I blink. Is this his way of getting me off in the woods to fill me full of lead? I swallow, not sure what to say.

"It's tradition. All the men in the family do it this time every year with the hunt club."

Is that his way of accepting me into the family? If so, I have to go, right? What other choice do I have other than to let him think I'm a little daughter-kissing pervert who's scared of big dogs? "Okay."

Lacie turns her head so quickly, I'm afraid I might have to pop her neck back in place. "You don't have to go."

"No, it's fine. I want to see this tradition."

Mr. Sanderson smiles for the first time. Well, at *me* for the first time. His face lights up like Christmas anytime someone mentions food . . . or Bradley.

"Great. Liam, take the boy upstairs and get him some camo."

I happily leave the dog monster and follow still-smelly Liam upstairs for a redneck makeover.

CHAPTER SEVEN

Collins

I leave the upstairs bathroom in head-to-toe camouflage. As skinny as Liam is, he was able to find enough clothing to fit me. And lucky for me, our feet are the same size.

I go to his bedroom door to take back the clothing that didn't fit. His room is covered with Auburn football posters, and he has a camouflage bedspread. Despite the mess, I spot a lone black ice skate in the corner. Little brat. I could've used that earlier.

"Thanks, man," he says, taking the stack of clothing and tossing it on the bed. Then he grabs a box of shells from the bedside table. "Let's go."

I follow him outside, noticing that he still hasn't showered from handling the pig. Mr. Sanderson stands at Liam's truck and fumbles at the backseat. "You'll want to get in on the other side, Collins." He shuts the back door and opens the front passenger one, then climbs inside.

I don't mind riding in the back. That is, until I open the door. I ease inside, careful not to touch any of the arsenal next to me.

"They're not loaded," Mr. Sanderson calls out from the front. I nod and give him a closed-lipped smile, happy for the heads up.

Liam jerks the truck in gear and barrels down the road like we're running from the law. I hug the door so that none of the guns slide into my legs. Mr. Sanderson's might not be loaded, but I don't trust Liam. Any kid who stands over a sleeping man with a knife and steals a skate is likely to mishandle a loaded gun.

When he screeches tires onto the main road, Mr. Sanderson finally corrects his driving. And then he keeps correcting it the entire trip. The two of them argue back and forth for half an hour, while I grip the handle above my door and keep an eye on the guns.

We bypass downtown Apple Cart and turn at the Gamers sign I saw on my way in. I'm beginning to wonder if this is some sort of virtual-reality shooting station. Maybe the guns aren't loaded after all. Though that wouldn't explain all the shells sitting on the console. Or that *were* on the console until Liam hung that final curve.

We bounce down a long dirt road. Again, I'm keeping my ear open for banjos. Instead, I hear a few faint gunshots in the distance. We pass a log mansion that has me in awe. Partly because it's impressive, and partly because who in the world would build something like that in this remote place? Then Liam parks by a line of other trucks.

We get out and walk toward a group of men standing in front of a pile of dirt. Most of them are wearing silencing earmuffs and glasses, and everyone is wearing camouflage. I feel like I've stumbled upon some sort of secret military-ops training. Maybe that mansion behind us is the base.

A man around Lacie's parents' age comes up to me and holds out his hand. I shake it.

"Earl Mayberry. You must be Lacie's guy."

"Nice to meet you, Mr. Mayberry, I'm Collins O'Conner."

"Please, call me Earl."

I smile at Earl and resist the urge to shoot a mean look at Joey—rather, Mr. Sanderson.

Earl gives my hand another tight grip, then releases it. I drop my hand behind my back and squeeze it into a fist to ease the numbness. He points to an overweight guy eating a Twinkie. "This is my son, Earl Ed." The guy nods and continues eating.

"Hi." I nod back, trying to remember where I've heard that name. Oh yeah, he's the Netflix thief. I study him a little closer. I'll bet he's a big Adam Sandler fan.

A more put-together guy my age stands next to him. He steps over and shakes my hand. "I'm Lacie's cousin, Michael."

"This is my other sister's oldest son," Earl points out. Then he fans his hand toward the larger group. "You'll meet these fools in a minute. They're the rest of our hunting club. That skinny feller over there is Jack. He owns this place."

Now it makes sense where I am. This must be the Jack who has a hunting camp and got the hog. "So we're here to hunt?"

"No, just shoot today," Mr. Sanderson corrects.

I almost ask why the need for all the camouflage, but I bite my tongue, yet again. I'm so going to need Orajel when this trip is over.

I follow Earl, Liam, and Mr. Sanderson to the dirt pile. A Christmas tree shape is spray painted in green, with red dots all inside of it. Some dots are smaller than others.

"The object of the game here, Collins, is to hit an ornament." Earl points the end of a rifle toward the tree and makes a clicking sound with his mouth. Then he lowers the gun and smiles. "What gun did you bring?"

I open my mouth to answer, but nothing comes out. Earl narrows his eyes at my dumbfounded silence. "Oh, you can use one of mine."

"Thanks."

Earl nods and leads me over to a truck bed loaded down with guns and ammo. I feel like I'm in a sporting goods store, except without the store. He points out all the different guns and goes over how they work. I nod and listen, as I don't want to come off like an idiot, although the closest thing I've used to a weapon is a scalpel in surgery.

Earl hands me a good "starter gun," as he calls it, and Mr. Sanderson agrees that it's a good choice. The other men in the family busy themselves picking out their guns, except for Earl Ed. He eats more snacks and mumbles something about not wanting to ruin his chances at living in the free world. That's understandable of anyone who's spent the last decade in the county jail.

All is well until an older, jacked-up Chevy parks beside Liam's truck. The door creaks open, and Bradley walks up. My body temperature rises as I wish with everything in me for him to go away. But my wishes never come true.

Bradley slaps his hand on my shoulder. "Hey there, Collins. I didn't expect to see you here."

"Same." My tongue is numb by now, so I had to let that one slip out.

"Bradley is really big in our gun club," Mr. Sanderson chimes in. That doesn't surprise me one bit.

Even Earl, my new friend in the family, steps toward Bradley and grins. "Bradley, I've been meaning to ask if you'll be the keynote speaker next month at the annual Alabama Gun Club banquet."

"Earl, I'd be honored." Bradley shakes his hand, then

grins at me. "When the president of the Alabama Gun Club says shoot, you pull the trigger."

Everyone around me starts laughing. I wasn't aware this was a joke, but I chuckle a little just to fit in. Not that it will help.

I listen to Bradley's bull a few more minutes, then the Jack guy steps up to the dirt and saves me. He points out all the dots on the tree and lets us know what size dots are worth how many points. "Jonah here will keep score."

A guy a little younger than me raises a notebook he's holding. Earl leans in and whispers, "That's Jack's little cousin. He helps out around here when he's home from college."

I nod. For the next hour, I watch men go head-to-head, or rather gun-to-gun, each trying to hit more points than the other. It's like observing a game of darts, except with guns, and dirt flying everywhere. Okay, so it's not so much like darts.

I'm content watching everyone else, until Earl puts a hand on my back. "It's your turn, son. Make me proud." I have no idea why he called me son or asked me to make him proud. We've just met. Then I catch a glimpse at Earl's own son eating Doritos and rapping the lyrics to a Luke Combs song. Okay, now I get it.

I step forward and relax my shoulders. Then I take the stance Earl described to me while everyone else shot, including himself. I concentrate on keeping a steady hand. If I can slice through someone's neck without hitting an artery, I should be able to hit a paint dot on a hill, right?

I exhale and pull back the trigger. And I hit the center target, worth a whopping fifty points. I fire off two more shots, hitting more targets. I want to do a victory dance but restrain myself.

Then Bradley steps up to the line. Ugh. I forgot he was

the only other person left. He fires off three shots quicker than a saloon showdown. And he outscores me by ten points. I curse under my breath and fire off three more. Then he fires. Jonah informs us that we're now tied.

Liam comes up behind me. "Hey, I've got a gun here that can beat him."

"For real?" I know Liam can't be trusted, but I can't let Bradley beat me.

"Yeah, here it is." Liam holds out a heavy gun and smiles. He puts it in my free hand and takes Earl's gun from me, then winks. Something doesn't sit well inside of me, but I'm desperate to outshoot this small-town sheriff.

I step up to the line and position the gun against my shoulder. As soon as I fire, it blasts into my arm. I lower the gun and grip my shoulder, half wondering if it's out of socket. Liam and Earl Ed burst out laughing.

"Liam, what did you do?" Mr. Sanderson turns around from chatting with other older men.

Liam turns pale and shakes his head. "Nothing, Daddy. I just let him borrow my gun."

"Which gun?"

Liam points slowly with his index finger, like a kid caught in the candy jar having to admit his wrong. Mr. Sanderson walks over and takes the gun from me. "Sorry about that, son."

Meanwhile, Bradley steps beside me and fires off three perfect shots. But who cares at this point? At least my throbbing shoulder is taking attention from my sore leg. And I think I'm finally bonding with Lacie's dad.

Lacie

"IS THIS ALL WE NEED?" I stare across the kitchen counter full of candy.

"Well, I could make more, but I know Carla's bringing cookies."

"Yeah, I think we're good." I glance back at the Crockpot full of macaroni and cheese, along with a pan full of biscuits. If anyone goes hungry tonight, it's their own fault.

G-Maw will have plenty of meats and vegetables, and Aunt Carla will bring her sweet-potato casserole and fried okra. Plus the cookies. Aunt Misty will bring herself, which is already more than enough.

I pull off tinfoil and start covering the candy trays. Mama won't let us bring them in Tupperware. We have to use the red and green platters. I agree that presentation is important, but I think she should consider her audience.

We hear the door to the garage open, then footsteps down the hallway. Daddy walks in with Collins, who's rubbing his shoulder, and Liam, who smells like pure crap.

Daddy kisses Mama on the cheek, then grabs a chocolate ball from one of the trays I haven't yet covered. "I'm gonna go take a shower," he says.

"That sounds like a good idea." Collins turns and starts toward the basement, still holding his shoulder. I don't know what happened out there, but it's like they're coming home from war.

Liam grabs an assortment of candies and sits at the kitchen table.

"No, sir, you go take a shower, too. You smell like that hog out there," Mama says.

He groans and rolls his eyes at her. Then he stands and picks up his plate. "Fine."

"Don't you sass me."

"Sorry," he mumbles as he leaves. I half expect a trail of dust to follow him like that kid on *Peanuts*.

I cover the rest of the candy before we lose any more to the guys, then I help Mama finish a few more tasks. Once everything is ready to take to dinner, I head toward the basement to check on Collins.

When I get downstairs, he's standing in the corner of the room, staring at something in his hand. "Collins?"

He jerks whatever it is from in front of his face and stares at me like a deer caught in the headlights. I frown. What could he be looking at to react that way? There's nothing that important in the basement, so I shrug it off. I probably scared him is all. He's been a little on edge ever since the parade.

"Are you okay?" I ask.

He smiles and walks over to me. "Yes." He wraps his arms around my waist, and I take a moment to admire how handsome he is. His light brown hair is still damp from his shower, and his eyes light up as he studies my face. I reach up and kiss him, but he pulls back.

What?" I wrinkle my forehead and frown.

"What if your dad comes down here?"

"We're nowhere near the bed. Besides, he's busy getting ready. Trust me, for an old redneck man, he takes his time primping.

Collins sighs and curves the corners of his mouth into a slight smile. I kiss him again, and this time he doesn't resist. Instead, he backs us up toward the mattress. He sits, pulling me onto his lap.

A loud yelp comes from behind us. It's Bully. He's probably mad that we're sharing the edge of the bed. Then Collins jumps, tossing me to the ground.

"What in the—"

"He bit me!" Collins clenches his teeth and rubs his backside.

I walk around to survey the damage. Sure enough, there's a huge rip in his khakis, with slobber outlining the tear. "Maybe he didn't mean to bite that hard?"

"Are you serious?"

I waver my head. "He only bites if something happens to him."

Collins rubs his butt and seethes. "Maybe I sat on his tail? I think he was turned that way when I sat us down."

"See, there you go."

He gives me a "go somewhere that isn't so pleasant" look. I overlook it in the name of pain and try to comfort him, but he hobbles toward the bathroom.

"I'm gonna change."

He grabs some pants and boxer briefs from his suitcase on the way, then slams the bathroom door behind him.

"Can I help with anything?" I call from outside the door.

"Can we kill that dog instead of the hog?" His voice is less sarcastic and more serious.

I pinch the bridge of my nose and sigh. "I'll go upstairs and let you change."

I stop by the bed and scold Bully. He shrinks his massive head down behind his front paws and whimpers. I shake my head and go upstairs.

Mama is still in the kitchen, wiping down the countertops from our cook-a-thon. I plop down on a stool in front of the island. I inhale, then exhale deeply, dropping my shoulders.

"Everything okay?" Mama asks.

I shrug. "Bully just bit Collins on the butt."

"What?" She drops her Mr. Clean sponge and puts a hand on her hip. "You're kidding me."

"Nope." I shake my head. "He sat on the edge of the bed, and Bully bit him."

"Well, now that's not like my Bully." Mama drops her gaze.

"Collins thinks he may have sat on his tail."

"Now that would make sense, a tail for a tail." I grimace at the sound of my brother's voice and look up to see him standing over the covered candy, wearing only shorts, and rubbing his head with a towel. At least he smells good now.

"That's not funny, Liam."

Liam shrugs and pinches the edge of the tinfoil. He starts to roll it back, but Mama swats his hand.

"I think you've had enough. Save some room for real food."

He draws his hand toward his chest and pouts. Then, he turns to me. "Lacie, if the guy's gonna make it around here, he needs to toughen up."

"Oh, is that why you gave him that gun?" Daddy steps in from the living room and folds his arms. Uh-oh, this must be serious. Liam's eyes dart around like he's searching for a way out.

"What gun?" I give Liam my sternest voice.

"Collins was a great shot. I just wanted to help him beat Bradley at the dirt-ornament game, that's all."

"What. Gun."

"The 577."

I pick up a potholder in front of me and chunk it at Liam's head. He flinches when it hits his face. "What? Daddy and I shoot it."

"He's not used to shooting like you two."

Daddy narrows his gaze on Liam. "I got on to him for it, Lacie Bug. Unfortunately, it was too late."

I sigh and toss back my head. "No wonder he came in rubbing his shoulder." I stare back at my family. "In two days' time, we've managed to hurt his leg, his shoulder, and thanks to Bully, his butt."

"What happened to his butt?"

I forgot Daddy wasn't in on this part of the conversation, so I catch him up to speed. "Bully bit Collins on the butt."

"That's not like Bully."

"Collins thinks he sat on his tail."

"Well, why would he do that?"

I drop my head in my hands, then lift my face back to Daddy. "It wasn't on purpose. He simply sat on the bed. And Bully's been wallowing all in his covers ever since you put him in the house."

"Oh my, I need to wash those sheets." Mama's face shows more concern about the dog on the bed than the dog biting Collins.

With nothing more to say, I retreat to the living room. I fall back onto the couch and pull the John Deere afghan over my legs. I'll wait here until Collins decides to come upstairs. That is, if he does decide to come upstairs. It's a walkout basement, so he may take this opportunity to get away. I know I would.

I've just settled on the couch when Mama darts into the room. I should've known. She can't leave well enough alone. I toss the throw over the back of the couch and rush toward my room. She follows me and makes it in my room before I can shut the door. She's awfully quick for a woman her age. Must be all the Zumba she does on her lunch breaks.

She puts a warm hand on my shoulder. "Lacie Bug, it's gonna be okay."

I shake my head and turn to face her. "Mama, this is exactly why I hadn't brought Collins home yet."

Worry lines form across Mama's pretty face. "Are you embarrassed of us?"

"No." I laugh. "Well, maybe Aunt Misty and Earl Ed, but not you guys."

Her face relaxes. "Then why?"

"Because I didn't want everyone to give him a hard time and run him off. You know how people are around here. They think anyone not born with a chew of tobacco in his mouth isn't a real man."

Mama's eyes move around my room as if she's hunting for words to say. Finally, she looks back at me. "Lacie, I can tell Collins is a good man and that he loves you and you love him. All your Daddy and I want is for you to find someone who will protect and love you and value the things we do."

I nod. "And I have all that with Collins."

"Then why are you so upset?"

I choke back a tear, then voice my biggest fear. "Because after all this, I don't know if he'll think I'm worth it."

CHAPTER EIGHT

Collins

I sit in the center of the couch, tapping my fingertips together. Liam stands in the corner of the room examining his knife, while Mr. Sanderson reads another section of the paper in his recliner. I debate making awkward small talk, but settle on staring at the animal busts in my peripheral vision.

At last, Lacie walks in with her mom. They've changed clothes, too, and both are carrying large cardboard boxes filled with bowls and foil-covered plates. I stand. "Let me help you."

"Thanks." Lacie hands me her box and smiles. Mr. Sanderson stands and takes the box from his wife. Liam stays in his corner as if he's in his own little world. I wonder what's going through his mind as he flicks his knife. Nah, I'd rather not know.

"Let's go to G-Maw's," Mrs. Sanderson announces, most likely to Liam, as she looks in his direction. He folds his Crocodile Dundee knife and slides it into a side pocket on his pants.

I follow Mr. Sanderson toward the door. Mrs. Sanderson opens it, then stops. "Wait, let me grab some tea." She disappears through the kitchen opening.

Liam rolls his eyes. "Why can't she just drink G-Maw's?"

"Because it's too sweet," Lacie answers.

Mrs. Sanderson strolls back from the kitchen with a gallon jug of Milo's Sweet Tea. "There. Mama's tea's so strong, your straw gets stuck in the middle."

If that's true, then I'm glad she grabbed the tea. Lacie motions for us to go on, and I follow Mr. Sanderson to his truck. We load the food on the back floorboard. I start to get in beside it, but Lacie pulls my arm. "We can ride separate in case we want to leave sooner than them."

"We can take the Land Rover."

She shrugs. "Okay."

"I just need my keys. Can you unlock the house to let me get them?"

"It's not locked."

I widen my eyes. I've noticed none of her family lock their vehicles, even in town, but this is extreme. These people have a lot of electronics . . . and guns.

When she doesn't laugh or say she's joking, I jog up to the house and go to the basement. I unzip the front of my suitcase and get my keys. As I turn to leave, my eye falls on the little black box. My stomach flips at the thought of presenting it to Lacie. Tomorrow is Christmas Eve. Time is winding down. I pick it up and start to put it in my pocket. Then I put it back in the security pocket inside my suitcase.

Before I make it upstairs, I hear Liam's truck fire up. He

must have a hard time sneaking in past curfew. I continue through the house and fight the urge to lock their door. It bothers me, even if it doesn't bother them.

Lacie waits patiently in the cold, bouncing on her toes and pulling her coat tighter. I unlock my doors, and she climbs inside. As I buckle my seat belt, I estimate how long it would take to get to a wedding chapel in Tennessee. An elopement would be perfectly fine with me . . . but Lacie deserves so much better than that.

I drop my shoulders and settle for driving a few miles to the end of the road to her grandparents' place. So many cars line the front lawn that we have to park near the RV at the edge of their yard. I'd noticed the lights before, but not so much the details of the decor. A plastic Santa sits in a sleigh pulled by six pink flamingos with reindeer antlers on their heads. Original.

We get out, and Lacie nods at the RV. "Woody will probably be at G-Maw's. He's rented an acre from them for about a year now. Oh, and he loves to get in the Christmas spirit." She taps a flamingo on the head and arches an eyebrow.

I laugh. "I can see."

We cross the gravel to her grandparents' yard. Lacie drops her gaze and pulls me back by my forearm. "Watch for poop."

"They have dogs?"

She shakes her head. "Goats."

"Don't you have to keep those in a pen?"

"They eat through it regularly. And these are tame."

"Oh." Like I know the difference between a tame and untame goat.

We make it to the porch without stepping in any poop. I take one step onto it, then lift my foot and glance around. The entire area is covered in AstroTurf.

"G-Maw is afraid of falling."

"Makes sense." I guess. There are no steps to the door, but instead a large ramp with rails. The rails have grips on them similar to a steering wheel cover. G-Maw must *really* be afraid of falling.

Lacie opens the screen door, and I stand back for her to go in first. I hear a bleat behind us and turn to see a goat eating a cactus plant. That's not good for either party involved. I ignore the goat and follow Lacie in the house.

I blink when the screen door slams behind me. Every eye turns toward the door and lands on me. I don't enjoy being the center of attention, especially if I'm quite certain it's negative attention. I swallow and force a nervous smile. "Hi."

They continue to stare in silence. Out of nowhere, two Chihuahuas run toward me, yapping and snipping at my feet. One is wearing a red sweater and the other a green one.

A man sitting in the corner of the room stands up and shakes his finger. "Taco, Belle, hush." Immediately, the two dogs cower down and rush to him. I don't know what it is about Wisteria, but these folks know how to make their dogs mind.

After another awkward moment of silence, Lacie clears her throat and says, "This is Collins, my boyfriend."

A tiny old woman comes shuffling toward us from behind a group of people. She stops in front of me and lifts her face, since the top of her gray head comes to my chest. She pushes her glasses up the bridge of her nose and squints, then she grins. "Welcome, Collins. I'm G-Maw."

She wraps her tiny arms around me and squeezes me tightly. It's like I'm being tackled by a peewee football player. Not knowing how to respond, I give her shoulder a gentle pat, then drop my arm as I wait for her to release me.

Once she does, she wraps an arm around Lacie's waist. "Honey, why don't you introduce everyone to Collins?"

Lacie nods. She bites her bottom lip and scans the room before speaking. I can't decide if she doesn't know everyone, or she just doesn't want me to know them. At last, she motions toward the left corner of the room.

"This is Woody. The neighbor right across the yard. He works with Daddy and Uncle Earl at the mines. And you've met his dogs, Taco and Belle."

Woody's mouth widens into a goofy grin. "Actually, they're my ex-wife's, but I get them on most holidays."

"Okay." Lacie nods and focuses her attention on the person beside him. "Sitting by Woody is Aunt Bea. She's G-Paw's older sister and lives a few miles from here off the main road." An old woman in a flowered dress sits in a rocker knitting something. She's like the personification of a nursery rhyme.

"Next to her is G-Paw." A man who looks like an older version of Earl darts his head around. "I said you're G-Paw," Lacie enunciates, speaking in a louder tone. He nods, then she points to me. "And this is Collins." He nods again. Lacie leans into me. "He can't hear all that well." No kidding.

"You've met Uncle Earl." Earl salutes me and winks. "This is Aunt Carla, his wife. She made the delicious cookies you had after the parade."

Carla smiles. She's older, but very pretty. Like a woman on a soap opera. "I made more cookies for tonight." She lifts her shoulders and smiles again. I smile back.

Lacie stands on her toes and looks around the room. "Earl Ed's around here someplace, but you've met him already, too." She points to a pretty teenager standing near the wall who's smacking gum and looking at pictures. "That's their daughter, Carly. She's still in high school." Carly continues smacking gum, but turns to us and smiles.

"Let's see, this is Aunt Misty." At the sound of her name, a blond woman dressed in some kind of red pantsuit struts over to us. This is the first time I've seen her, so I'm not sure when she came in the room.

"Well, hello." She extends a manicured hand, and I shake it. She bats her fake eyelashes so hard, I swear they'll stick together. "You sure know how to pick them, Lacie." She giggles like a school girl, then slings her hair over her shoulder and struts over to Woody.

Lacie simply moves on with the introductions as if that interaction never happened. "Aunt Misty's kids are all around. You met Michael yesterday. He's the oldest." Michael waves at me, and I raise a hand to him.

"I don't see Tommy here. But that's Ashton." Lacie points to another teenage girl who's slumped on the edge of the couch, staring at her phone. She's pretty, too, but in a much edgier way. And by the way she's dressed, I'm assuming she hasn't checked the weather report in a few months.

"The little boys running around are Ricky and Conner." Lacie motions toward the back of the house as a boy runs by. He's wearing a baseball cap and a gold chain. "And the baby is Piper." Lacie points toward Woody, who is now holding a toddler girl and making funny faces at her.

"Then . . ." Lacie stops and cocks her head at the woman beside Michael. "I'm sorry, I don't think we've met."

A blond girl with a huge pregnant belly walks up to us. Or at least I'm assuming it's a pregnancy, judging by her otherwise small stature. But in the medical field, I've made the mistake of making assumptions one too many times.

"I'm Krystal, Michael's fiancée." She rubs her belly, which leads me to believe she must be pregnant.

Lacie glances back at her cousin. "Congratulations, Michael."

He shakes his head. "It's not mine."

Lacie pinches her lips shut and looks at me. I'm pretty

sure she meant the engagement and not the baby. But at least Michael cleared that up.

Krystal rushes over to Michael and wraps her arms around him. "Don't say that, pumpkin. You'll still be my baby daddy, and you'll be a great one."

"Thanks, babe." Michael smiles at her, and within a second they're making out. This is awkward for just about everyone, except Earl Ed, who tries to start a slow clap. Come on, dude. This isn't a John Hughes movie.

Earl steps to the center of the room and lets out a loud whistle. At least that breaks apart the lovebirds. Once he has everyone's attention, he says, "Okay, how about we say the blessing and eat."

Collins

"DEAR FATHER IN HEAVEN, we thank you for this wonderful holiday season. We pray that you bless this food and bless our hunts so that we can continue to provide more food for our families. We thank you for our freedom, most of all for the right to bear arms. In your name we pray, amen."

The entire room mutters "amen" in unison, and I join in just a tad too late. I don't always pray before I eat, but I have been praying lately. Between going to church each week with Lacie and literally going into life and death situations at work, it seems like the right thing to do. However, Earl's prayer marks the first time I've ever heard anyone thank God for guns.

As soon as the "amen" ends, people scatter in every direction. I turn to Lacie, not sure what's going on.

"It's best to just hang back and wait." She stays planted near the door, and so do I. We wait until the only person left in the living room is Aunt Bea. She's rocking away, knitting and humming the national anthem. Earl's speech must've sparked some patriotism in her.

Lacie takes my hand and leads me out of the living room. We make it to a hallway, where everyone is lined against the wall. Someone hands us some Styrofoam plates and plastic silverware. After the line progresses a few feet, I start to see food.

We walk through and fix our plates. I haven't seen this much food at once since my grandparents took me to Golden Corral as a kid. I'm halfway expecting to find a chocolate fountain at the end of it all. We wrap around a countertop and small kitchen island before everything ends.

No chocolate fountain, but I was close. It's a card table filled with all the candies Lacie and her mom have been making, plus decorative cookies and some cakes. I pray nobody is allergic to chocolate . . . or sugar.

Mrs. Sanderson and Carla stand behind another card table with a cooler of ice. One fills red Solo cups with ice, while the other pours the drinks.

"What would you like to drink, Collins?" Carla asks me with a smile.

"Sweet tea is fine."

Mrs. Sanderson reaches under the table and pulls out her jug of Milo's tea. "You'll want this one, or else you'll go into a diabetic coma."

"Thanks." I laugh a little as she pours my cup, then returns the jug to the floor. I wonder if her mom knows she's smuggling store-bought tea to this dinner.

Lacie gets her drink, then nods back at the dessert table. "You might want to grab something you really want in case it's gone before you finish the main course."

I blink at the massive selection of sweets. How could there possibly not be anything left? Lacie reaches over me and piles a paper plate with some of her mom's candies and aunt's cookies. She smiles at me. "You'll thank me later." Then she stacks the dessert plate on her cup like a pro and walks toward the dining room.

The dining room table is full, as are the two chairs in the corner of that room, and the piano bench beside it. She leads me back to the living room, where the couch and chairs are all taken.

"Ugh. I took too long picking cookies." Lacie groans and leads me back to the other side of the kitchen. Nobody is at the table except for Misty and Woody. Lacie sits across from them, and I sit beside her. A minute later, Michael and Krystal join us.

A blast of cold air hits my backside, causing the hairs on my neck to raise. I turn and see a window-unit air conditioner shooting tiny ice crystals my way. I shudder, then turn back to my plate.

"Hey, Collins, do you mind if Krystal has your seat?" Michael asks. Krystal stands beside him, fanning herself with a paper plate.

"Not at all." I go sit on the other side of Lacie, happy to put the pregnant lady in the arctic circle.

Squeezing past the crowd to the end of the table poses a challenge for Krystal and her belly, but she makes it through. She plops down in front of the air and sighs. "That feels amazing."

She kicks her shoes off and props her feet up in the windowsill beside the box unit. Nobody says a word. Lacie scoots her chair closer to mine and slides her plate farther from Krystal's feet. We all start eating.

Michael must sense that the elephant in the room is his

very pregnant fiancée, because he starts talking. "Woody, how old are Taco and Belle?"

Woody grins. "They're two and a half. I got them for my ex-wife on our anniversary. She'd been eying Chihuahuas for a while. Then I found out a week later that she'd been cheating on me with the dog breeder."

I almost choke on my turkey and have to take a huge gulp of tea. Mrs. Sanderson pouring me Milo's instead of the solid sugar in most everyone else's cups might've just saved my life.

"That's horrible," Lacie comments between bites of macaroni and cheese.

"Yeah, but I guess it's for the best. We never had any kids besides Taco and Belle, and she's great about letting me get them for holidays and some weekends."

Lacie smiles, then takes a sip of her tea. Woody returns her smile, then looks at Misty. "And Misty's kind enough to let me babysit Piper whenever I'm off work."

Lacie clears her throat. "I bet she is."

Before Lacie can slather on any more sarcasm, the doorbell rings. Someone yells from another room, "I'll get it." We resume eating, and Krystal finally drops her feet. Michael pushes a plate in front of her, and she forks the potatoes like her life depends on it.

A guy wearing an Atlanta Braves cap and shirt, along with a gold chain, steps up to our table. He stares at Misty. She stares back for a second, then asks, "What?"

"I'm here to get the boys."

"They just got here thirty minutes ago."

"That's not my problem."

"Let them finish eating."

He twists his arm and checks a large gold watch. "Can't. We got travel ball at nine tomorrow."

"On Christmas Eve?" Misty cocks her head to call his bluff.

"Yeah, it's championship tournaments. You'd know that if you ever came to a game."

Misty huffs. "It's not like I don't have four other kids to keep up with."

"Not my problem."

Woody pushes back his chair and stands. I expect him to go get dessert, but instead, he looks at the overgrown baseball guy. "Can't the boys at least finish their meal?"

The guy sizes Woody up, then sniffs. "Guess so, if I can have one of those deer-head cookies." He nods at the dessert plate Lacie made for us. On top of everything is a cookie of a deer wearing a Christmas sweater and a Santa hat, with ornaments hanging from its antlers. Lacie starts to pull back the plate, but I don't like this guy being here. I snatch the cookie and hand it to him. "Here."

"Thanks, man." He puts out a fist. Either he's trying to slow-motion punch me or he wants a fist bump. I bump his fist, then let out the breath I'm holding when that satisfies him.

He bites the antlers off the cookie and walks out of the kitchen. Misty seethes as she watches him leave. Then she reaches behind her and picks up Piper, who's toddling through the kitchen. Piper spots Woody and reaches for him. It's my guess that Woody's a much more attentive babysitter than Misty is a parent. The way he got those tiny dogs to get off my feet has to mean something.

Travel-ball dad has really put a damper on the mood. We all look around and pick at our food. Except for Krystal, who's never slowed down eating. I decide to try and clear the air by getting to know these people better. If there's one thing I've learned in my twenty-seven years, it's that people like to talk about themselves.

"Michael, how did you meet Krystal?"

Krystal stops eating for the first time and smiles. Michael takes her hand and perks up before answering. "It was back in the summer when Earl Ed first got out of jail. I picked him up and asked him what the first thing was that he wanted to go do."

Michael laughs to himself, then shakes his head. "That fool wanted to go to Tunica to the casinos."

I catch a glimpse of Lacie out of the corner of my eye. She's tracing the outline of a cookie with her plastic fork, but I know she's listening. She has a habit of fidgeting with things when people talk.

"I do my boy Earl Ed right. We go to the biggest casino. You know the one with the crab legs at the buffet and those moving tracks where you don't have to walk?"

I nod, even though I have no clue where he's talking about.

"We play the slots awhile, then Earl Ed decides he wants to win enough to get a free meal. I suggest we play blackjack to expedite our earnings. We sit at the blackjack table and this beautiful blonde walks up and sits beside us." Michael nudges Krystal, and she blushes.

"That was Krystal?" Lacie asks.

"Nope."

Lacie and I exchange a confused look.

"But then, another hot blonde comes up to take drink orders, and that was Krystal."

Krystal starts to giggle. "The whole night, I thought Michael was with the blonde playing blackjack. That is, until she got up and left with the old man sitting across from them."

"So what happened when you knew he wasn't with her?" Lacie asks.

"Earl Ed asked me out, but he isn't my type." Krystal

scrunches her nose. It's refreshing for me to know that despite working in a casino and being pregnant with a baby by someone other than her fiancé, she wouldn't lower her standards to an ex-criminal.

Michael grins widely. "She politely turned him down, then asked if I was there with someone. I, of course, said I was, thinking she meant Earl Ed."

Lacie raises her eyebrow at me, no doubt wondering how they ever got on the same page.

"She smiled and left then. So we finally get enough money for a free meal, and even enough for a free room. Earl Ed and me go eat at the buffet, play some more slots, then go to bed. The next day as we're going out, we see her coming in to work."

Krystal bats her eyes at Michael. "I knew I had to ask him out before he left. So I asked if he'd ever dated a pregnant woman before."

"I said not that I knew about." Michael slaps the table and laughs.

"Then I asked if he'd consider it. 'Cause if you're pregnant, showing or not, the right thing to do is tell a man."

Lacie and I exchange a smirk.

Michael nods. "After she explained her boyfriend left her when he found out about the baby, it made me mad. Who'd leave someone pretty and sweet like her? I told her that, and she asked if we'd stick around town until she got off that night. So we played a little more while she worked, then we all went out for hot wings."

Krystal leans her head on Michael's shoulder. "And before they left town, he took me in the jewelry store at the casino and told me to pick out a ring."

Lacie gives Krystal the face she gives someone when she's half happy and half sorry for them. "When's the wedding?"

Krystal raises her eyes to the ceiling. "Oh gosh, I haven't

decided." She looks back at us and grins. "I'm due end of January, so I want to wait until I can fit into a mermaid gown." She outlines her belly with her palms.

Lacie nods, then cuts her eyes at me. I try not to laugh. Luckily, G-Maw hobbles in, yelling for everyone's attention.

CHAPTER NINE

Lacie

G-Maw stops in front of the kitchen entrance and claps her hands until everyone stops talking. I hear familiar lines from *Christmas Vacation* coming from the living room TV. "Mute that, Ed." She waits a minute, then shakes her head. She yells again. "Ed, mute!" G-Paw heard her that time, because the noise cuts out right before Cousin Eddie announces what's full.

"We're all gathering in the den to play Dirty Santa in five minutes. You can bring food in there if you'd like. But if anyone else has a gift to add, let me know." She shoves a piece of paper and a pen my direction. "Lacie's gonna write out numbers."

I have no idea who plans to play or how many. But G-Maw always keeps extra gifts on hand so that anyone coming in late feels welcome to play. That's why I start writing numbers before asking.

Krystal leans across the table to get my attention. "Lacie, my name is spelled with a 'K,' like the restaurant."

"Thanks, but I'm just writing numbers." I hold up the paper so Krystal can see. She giggles and nods.

I write numbers all the way to forty just in case, as G-Maw starts herding anyone thirteen and older to the den. It's two steps down off the kitchen, with a fireplace and chairs all around. The middle of the room is vacant, making it the perfect place to set all the gifts.

Aunt Carla and Mama walk around the house, making sure every gift marked "Dirty Santa" is in that room. We implemented mandatory marking of Dirty Santa gifts the year Michael opened a nightgown someone had bought for G-Maw. I laugh to myself at the memory of a teenage boy opening a plaid nightgown made for a tiny old lady. The good news was G-Maw ended up stealing it even before someone discovered the mishap. So at least the person who brought it knew she liked it.

I stand and grab a pair of scissors from the junk drawer inside the kitchen island, along with a Solo cup from the counter.

I hear G-Maw loud and clear from the living room. "Jeffrey, do you want to play?"

I can't believe she just asked Aunt Misty's ex to play, or that he's still here. I'd assumed after he walked off with my reindeer cookie that he gave up on getting the boys tonight.

"Twenty-five, Lacie!" G-Maw calls out.

"Yes, ma'am." I cut off all the numbers through twenty-five. Then I fold them all in half one by one, tossing them into the plastic cup.

G-Maw comes back into the kitchen and points to Collins. "And he will make twenty-six."

I glance at Collins, who shakes his head. Wise choice. I

turn to G-Maw. "I don't think either of us wants to play this year."

"Now that is nonsense." G-Maw props her hands on her hips.

Collins shakes his head. "Thanks, but I didn't bring a gift."

G-Maw puts a feeble hand on his shoulder. "It's okay. We have extra."

I smile, trying to hide my amusement at what those extra gifts entail. Knowing G-Maw, it's some sort of lotion from Bath & Body Works or a gourmet soup mix she picked up at the farmer's market.

Collins scans the room as if looking for an escape. G-Maw pats his broad shoulder and smiles when he looks at her. With him sitting, they're almost eye to eye. At this point, I'm just along for the ride. Who can say no to G-Maw?

Collins sighs and stands. He looks at me, and I cut off numbers twenty-six and twenty-seven, then toss them into the cup as well. We cross the kitchen and step down into the den. G-Maw stands at the threshold, fanning people that way. Once everyone has made it in the den, she grabs hold of the doorframe and eases herself down.

When I was in college, G-Maw fell and broke her hip. It was the Fourth of July and someone had dumped a cooler of ice in the driveway. She slid on some of the ice and ended up needing a hip replacement. The next month, she hired the turf management company out of Tuscaloosa that fixed the Apple Cart Baptist Church soccer field to come out and cover every inch of concrete and wood outside her home. Someone from out of town stopped by once thinking her house was a mini-golf course.

We find some seats near the corner of the room. Collins sits down slowly and shifts to his side. I touch his arm and ask, "Are you okay?"

He nods. "Yeah, the wood on this chair isn't agreeing so well with my dog bite wound is all." We're stuck with some chairs from the former dining set that don't have cushions.

"We can move." Instead of waiting for him to answer, I take his hand and lead him to the other side of the room. We take a seat on a huge camouflage-print beanbag.

Misty's youngest boy runs up and crosses his arms. "That's my Christmas present from G-Maw."

Collins starts to stand, but G-Paw intervenes. "Connor, let the man borrow it, or I'll take it back." Conner sulks a second, then drops his head and walks away.

G-Maw catches him at the doorway. "Why don't you go play with your brother?" As soon as G-Maw releases him, he bolts for the door. We hear the TV come back on in the living room.

Uncle Earl stands and clears his throat, then spouts off the rules to the game. I survey the room to see who all is now here to drive our number up to twenty-seven. Misty's oldest boy, Tommy. Carly's boyfriend is here now, too. He's sitting between Carly and Ashton, which probably isn't wise on Carly's part.

Some of the neighbors from down the road are here. I'm not sure if they came while we were eating or after. They have seven kids and all are homeschooled. They're fascinated with my family's events, especially the hog killing. They even count attending it and helping grind sausage as part of their science curriculum each year. The older kids are in the den, ready to play.

Oh, and who can forget that Jeffrey is still here? Nobody's seen him in four years until tonight, but he's happy to eat all the best cookies and play Dirty Santa.

Some people question the validity of getting number one, even though we play this same game the same way every year. But Uncle Earl is more than happy to correct them. He's overly passionate about two things in life: gun laws and Dirty Santa.

At last, G-Paw tells Earl to get on with it and prompts me to pass out numbers. I give it a gentle shake and start around the room. I know better than to pull the first number. Since I wrote them out, everyone will say it's rigged if I get a number they want.

When I get to the center of the room, Paul, the General Store owner, is standing in the doorway. I must've missed him earlier. I hold the cup in front of him, but he shakes his head and lifts a Styrofoam box. "I just stopped in for some food." Of course, he did. He's known for popping in anytime and anywhere there's food for a free meal. I continue on with the cup and end back at Collins, then pick the last number for me.

I draw out twenty, which is pretty pathetic. But Collins gets number two, which is the worst number possible, according to Uncle Earl's rules. I'm actually glad, so nobody can say I rigged the game.

We start with Jeffrey, who got number one. A few people shoot him the evil eye, since none of us like him anyway. He gets a battery-powered flashlight and complains that it doesn't come with batteries. But it's hard to work with a ten-dollar spending cap.

We go through the next gifts fairly quickly, until someone opens a gift card to Tractor Supply. You'd think that ten dollars was gold the way the men swap for it. Daddy ends up with it last and proudly tucks it in his shirt pocket, declaring it "dead."

I get a bottle of cherry-blossom scented lotion, which I'm sure is compliments of G-Maw's closet stash. Hey, it could be worse. Aunt Bea is after me and shakes her skinny finger toward a small bag near the fireplace. Liam picks it up and takes it to her. She sets her knitting aside and opens it. She pulls out a clear box that reveals two sparkly circles with tassels hanging from them. She smiles best she can for someone who isn't wearing her teeth. She opens the box, tosses it to the floor, and laughs.

Collins leans toward my ear. "Is that what I think it is?"

I catch a glimpse at the box, now in the middle of the floor. The words "Ta-Ta Tassels" are prominently displayed at the top. "I'm afraid so."

Aunt Bea tries to stick them to her ears but they fall down. Earl Ed speaks up. "That's not where those go, Aunt Bea."

G-Maw glares at Earl Ed, as if just now realizing this gift is what the rest of us feared it was all along. "Did you bring these?"

"No." Earl Ed shakes his head. I'm not sure I believe him. He could've ordered them from Victoria's Secret for all we know.

Krystal raises her hand slowly, as if she's a student unsure of an answer to the teacher's question. "I brought them." Then she hangs her head and cries. "I'm so sorry. Michael said y'all play Dirty Santa."

Michael rubs her shoulders. "Honey, it's okay."

Krystal shakes her head and sobs. "I just thought since you said everyone over thirteen."

I press my lips together. I don't know in what world something like that would be appropriate for a fourteen-year-old, or anyone for that matter. But I can't say I'm surprised. Many odd characters have come through G-Maw's house on a holiday. And this Christmas happens to be a full moon. That is, until those snow clouds cover it.

Aunt Bea holds up one of the tassels and spreads out the strings, watching them fall. She's oblivious to what we're discussing, and she obviously likes her gift.

Collins clears his throat. "That's a great gag gift, Krystal."

She sniffles and curves her lips into a slight smile. Collins looks at Bea and speaks loud enough for her to hear. "Aunt Bea, those will look great knitted onto a scarf."

Aunt Bea's cheeks lift and her mouth widens to reveal her gums. Collins stands and goes over to Bea and takes one of the tassels. He places it against her knitting project. "See."

Bea grins wider and claps her hands. Earl Ed starts clapping, and then Michael and Krystal, and soon everyone else joins in applause. After years of failed attempts, Earl Ed has managed to start a slow clap. Well, technically Aunt Bea did.

All I can think about in that moment are two things. I have an extremely thoughtful boyfriend, and I'd hate to be the parents of those homeschool kids when they start asking questions about Aunt Bea's gift.

Collins

I'D LIKE to say I can't believe that my girlfriend's cousin's pregnant fiancée brought an adult accessory for the family Christmas gift swap. But after a few days in Wisteria, I'd about believe anything.

Dirty Santa ended on a high note, with only one more hiccup. Jeffrey tried to steal the tassels from Aunt Bea since he got number one. We wouldn't allow it, though, as she'd already managed to knit some of the sequins into her yarn. Besides, I don't think his intentions for them were as innocent as hers.

As soon as the game ended, Jeffrey tucked his quesadilla maker under his arm and said we were all cheaters. Then he gathered his sons and left. Nobody seemed to mind.

Conner took away my bean bag chair on their way out, leaving me without a comfortable seat. So I volunteered to help G-Maw wash dishes.

"Here you go." G-Maw hands me another pot large enough to feed an army. I dry it off and set it aside.

Earl Ed, Michael, and Liam sit at the kitchen table, shuffling a stack of Rook cards. All the women except Misty and Aunt Bea busy themselves throwing away plates and cups from around the house and covering up leftovers. I continue my drying duty as I listen to them chat in the background.

"I can take the rest of this cake to work Monday if nobody wants it," Mrs. Sanderson calls out to the rest of the women.

"Where do you work?" Krystal asks as she stands beside me, pouring watered-down drinks into the sink.

"At the University of Alabama."

Krystal's eyes bug, and she stops what she's doing. "Do you work with Nick Saban?"

Mrs. Sanderson laughs. "No, I manage the AA department."

"Oh, really? I went to those meetings for a few years."

Michael speaks up. "No, babe. Not your kind of AA. The alumni association."

"Oh." Krystal blushes and continues tossing out ice. I offer her a half-smile to try and ease her nerves. I sympathize with her, being the new person here. And I'm not the one who brought a dirty gift.

Aunt Bea shuffles into the kitchen and holds up a yellow scarf, complete with the red tassels knitted into the center. Lacie and Carla compliment her work. She smiles and nods. Michael tells her "great job," and she turns toward his voice.

Then her eyes go dark as she narrows them on the kitchen table. She shakes her knitting needles toward the cards and chants, "Evil, evil, evil."

"Bea, it's just Rook, not poker." G-Maw wipes the sudsy water from her hands and walks up to her. That doesn't help. Bea shakes her needles even faster and yells, "Cards are evil."

G-Maw reaches for her needles to try and calm her down. But Aunt Bea points them at G-Maw and says, "Don't." Then she storms out of the room.

Nobody says a word for several minutes. We hear the front door shut, followed by a truck cranking.

"Oh dear." G-Maw moves back to the sink and pulls over the floral curtain. Taillights shine through the window. "She always leaves when she gets mad. I'll call her house in a bit and make sure she got in okay."

G-Maw shakes her head and closes the curtain. She resumes her washing, and I continue drying. There are so many pans that I now have to stack them pyramid style on the narrow countertop.

Carly walks in with Misty's daughter and comes up to Carla. "Mama, we're going to see Christmas lights with Andrew and some more friends."

"Not dressed like that you aren't."

I can't resist turning completely around to see what's caused calm Carla to use such a tone. Carly is wearing a shirt that's more the length of a bra and jeans with holes in a lot of places.

"Where did you get those clothes?"

"They're some Ashton brought."

"We've discussed this. Just because Ashton wears it doesn't mean you do."

Ashton looks up from her phone just long enough to roll her eyes at Carla. Carly droops her shoulders and lets out a dramatic sigh. "But Mama!"

"No, ma'am. You're better than that."

Ashton folds her arms and scoffs. "Here we go again.

Perfect Carly can't be in style." She leaves the room, bumping Carla on the shoulder as she does.

Carla shakes her head. "I swear, that child."

"Aunt Carla, if you think Ashton dresses bad, you should see the girls at Auburn." Liam laughs.

Both Carla and Mrs. Sanderson glare at Liam. His face reddens. "Not that I look or anything."

Carla turns back to Carly. "Go change, and be home by eleven."

Carly nods. "Yes, ma'am." She starts out of the room, but Carla calls after her, "And Carly?" She twists her head toward her mom. "Leave Ashton here." Carly frowns and nods.

Liam tosses his cards on the table and hops up. "I can go with them. You know, for a chaperone."

Carla gives him a skeptical look, but doesn't say anything. I'm guessing when it comes to Ashton and Liam, he's the lesser of two evils.

"Collins, you play Rook?" Earl Ed asks. I'm impressed at how he can speak so clearly and keep the toothpick in his mouth from moving.

"I can."

"Good, you can take Liam's spot when we start to play."

"Who's our fourth?" Michael shuffles the stack and looks at Earl Ed.

"We'll get Daddy or that boy from down the road, I guess."

Michael shrugs. I dry the last of the dishes that have piled up while I witnessed the dress-code debacle. Then I go take a seat at the kitchen table. Michael continues shuffling a million different ways. He even does that thing where you pull your hands apart and let the cards flow down like an accordion. I wonder if he learned that from Krystal. Maybe she could be our fourth. Nah, I like to win.

Earl Ed and Michael are still debating who they want to

play when we hear a gust of wind, then the screen door slam shut. Everyone focuses on the kitchen entrance that leads to the hallway. We can hear heavy boots, then a cowboy hat appears from the shadows.

I know exactly who it is, and I don't like it.

"Evening, Mayberry family." Bradley tips his hat like some dude in a spaghetti western.

I fight the urge to roll my eyes. For a split second, I wish Ashton would come back and do it for me.

"I just wanted to let y'all know I saw Aunt Bea's truck parked close to the Waffle House. I stopped and checked on her. She said the winds were so strong, she didn't like driving in them. So I took her home and told her we could get her truck to her house by the morning. Here are the keys." He lays a set of keys on the kitchen counter.

"Thank you, Bradley. I'll have Earl or Joey ride with you to the truck. But would you like some tea and cookies first?" G-Maw says.

No, say no.

"Yes, ma'am, I'd love some."

Dang it. Of course he wants to stay.

"Hey, Bradley, why don't you join us?"

Bradley unzips his jacket and sits across from me. "Thanks, Earl Ed."

I drop my eyes toward the poinsettia-print table cloth, not liking my new view. Mr. Sanderson is warming up to me, and we're all having a nice family Christmas. A strange one, but a nice one. Then big, bad Brad swoops in to ruin it.

Michael does another fancy shuffle move, then asks Earl Ed to cut the cards. Earl Ed does so, then passes them out. He leaves a few for the middle stack and flips the top card over.

"I guess we're partners since we're sitting across from one another." Bradley flashes a smile my way, and it's all I can do to not knock the table over on him. But I'm trying to be the better man. I ask myself, *What would Jesus do?* Then I remember that he turned some tables over one time in the temple. I place my fingertips under the edge of the table.

I can't do it.

Lacie is standing nearby laughing with her mom and aunt. And I'd hate to scuff G-Maw's furniture. Instead, I remember the time I heard a sermon about killing people with kindness or something like that. So I smile back. "Yep."

But I'm still new to church, so I can't help but want to outbid Bradley, even though we're on the same team. A red six stares at us from the top of the stack. It's nothing to bid on, and my own hand resembles a bag of Skittles. But I'm dying to taste whatever rainbow is inside that stack, just so Bradley can't have control.

We go around bidding, and I keep quiet until the other team stops, then I up Bradley's final bid by ten. It's way too high, and I'm not at all confident we can pull this off. But I'll dang sure try.

Bradley shakes his head and raises his eyebrows at the stack. "Take it away, big dog."

I rake the cards my way as if I'm raking in a million poker chips. Instead, I've got a bunch of fives and a single one card. And it's also a rainbow, just like I predicted.

With few points, no Rook, and no dominant color, I scratch my beard and contemplate what I'll do for trumps. I call green, which is my only one card, then discard some of the other colors. Here we go. No pressure.

The first few sets are rough, as I'm clinging to my one for dear life. Bradley gets a drag and takes control. To my delight, he has some high-point green cards. The hairs on my neck stop bristling and I decide to let him lead.

Earl Ed has the Rook, which takes some key cards. We

now need to win every set to win the game. I grip my remaining cards and pray that Bradley can pull us through.

Maybe God will hear me, even though I wanted to do bad things to my game partner a few minutes earlier.

I look up from my cards to see that Lacie, Carla, Mrs. Sanderson, and G-Maw are all focused on our game. Bradley wins another set, and I relax my shoulders. He tosses out a crap card for the final round. I laugh, as I still have my green one. I toss it down, and Earl Ed groans.

We win by the skin of our teeth. Lacie comes over and kisses me. The rest of the women clap and congratulate us. Bradley even stands and offers his hand. I shake it and give him a face that communicates my joy in knowing Lacie is latched onto me and not him.

"Well, Mayberrys, I best get back to my patrolling." Bradley grabs the keys off the counter and waves a hand as he exits the kitchen. Everyone tells him "bye." Bradley goes into the living room, and we can hear him explaining the truck situation. Earl offers to ride and pick it up. Then there's another gust of air, and the screen door slams behind them.

Lacie smiles at me. "Hear that wind?" I nod. "It's gonna snow tomorrow." I laugh. She's cute when she's delusional.

CHAPTER TEN

Lacie

I hug G-Maw one more time before stepping out onto the front porch. Collins follows behind me, carrying two plates of turkey dressing and half a pecan pie. Neither of us wanted to take it home, especially since we're going back to Mama's. But I can't find it in my heart to tell G-Maw no.

We make our way down the AstroTurf and through the yard. It's easier to see the grass now, because the porch light is on. I hear one of the goats nearby in the trees, then laughter as we walk closer to the SUV.

Aunt Misty stands at the edge of Woody's yard, smoking a vape. That's probably her brilliant solution to G-Maw repeatedly telling her that cigarettes are bad for her and that she can never smoke in her yard. Woody chats with her from a few feet away, where he has Taco and Belle on leashes, letting them do their business.

I drop my gaze, hoping they won't notice me noticing

them. Either they don't, or they don't care. They continue laughing and ignore us. We put the food in the backseat, then get in.

Collins turns on the heater and blows into his hands. I buckle my seat belt and peer out the windshield. "See those clouds coming in? It's all coming together for the winter storm."

He laughs. "I hope it flurries just for you, my dear."

I huff and cross my arms. "It's gonna do more than that. You just wait and see."

"Okay . . ." He backs out of the yard and starts down the short drive leading to the road back to Mama's house.

"Hey, Collins. Thanks for being so nice to everyone."

"Of course." He frowns at me. "Why wouldn't I be nice?"

I shrug and tuck a strand of hair behind my ear. "I don't know. My family can get a little weird."

"Every family has some weirdness."

"Yours doesn't." I say that to myself, but he hears me all the same.

"Yes we do. I'm an only child and only grandchild, and all my grandparents are dead. My whole life, Christmas has been Mom, Dad, and me watching *A Christmas Story* while he grills steaks on the patio."

I laugh. "That sounds low-key and amazing."

He wavers his head. "You know, you'd think so, but it gets pretty mundane and boring."

Despite all that's happened this week, I'm really happy right now. I rest my hand on Collins's knee and smile. He wraps his hand around mine and smiles back. We lock eyes for a few seconds, then I face the road just in time to see a huge buck running in front of us. I scream at the top of my lungs, "Stop!"

Collins slams on the brakes and swerves to the right. Just when I think we're going to miss it, I hear metal popping on

Collins's side of the vehicle. We slide a few feet, then land with our front wheels in the ditch.

My heart pounds a million miles a minute. Once I catch my breath, I turn to Collins. "Are you okay?"

He looks down at his legs and hands, then nods at me. "Yeah, you?"

"Yeah, just shook up."

He strokes the side of my face, and I put my hand on his and lift the corner of my mouth. He squeezes my hand, then drops his. He pulls his door handle, but the door doesn't open. After a few hard jerks, he gives up. I unbuckle my seat belt and lean behind his seat. The side of the back door is bent in, and I'm pretty sure the food from G-Maw's spilled.

"I think the deer messed up your side."

Collins sighs and swipes his hands down his face. I scoot over and hug him. He falls onto my shoulder and sighs again. I hear Liam's truck in the distance and perk up. "Liam can pull us out of this ditch."

Collins raises his head and gives me a confused look. "Your Liam?"

I nod. "Yeah."

I open my door and hop out, waving my arms as Liam drives toward us. He stops and gets out. "Whoa, what happened here?"

"We hit a buck."

Liam walks around the front of the SUV and bends down. "Yep, you killed it, too." He stands and turns back toward his truck. Carly and two of her friends are inside. "Hey, ladies, critter, critter." Liam smiles and wiggles his eyebrows.

I go over and punch him in the arm.

He rubs his arm. "What was that for?"

"You shouldn't be playing critter, critter, especially with high school girls. Especially with your cousin!"

"What's critter, critter?"

I look toward Collins's voice. He's standing up through the moonroof. "It's a stupid game where you hunt for road-kill, and the last person to say 'critter, critter' loses a piece of clothing."

He looks at Liam. "Yeah, you shouldn't play that with your cousin. That's creepy."

Liam stares at his boots as if he's finally realizing how creepy that is.

"So, can you pull us out with your winch?" I ask.

He pulls his cap down and frowns at the front of the SUV. "Yeah, I think so. Get everyone out."

I nod. "Collins, come on." I motion toward the road, then go to Liam's truck and tell the three girls to get out. The five of us stand back while Liam pulls up to the Land Rover and hooks his winch to the front.

I have everyone back up even more when he gets back in his truck. Liam puts his truck in reverse and slowly pulls it into the road. He gets out and unhooks everything, then looks under the vehicle. "Looks like the tires are fine. You just need to get this big dent fixed."

Collins nods. "Thanks."

"Sure thing." Liam glances at the ditch. "What you plan on doing with the deer?"

Collins shrugs. "Leave it there?"

"Mind if I take it off your hands?"

Collins lifts his hands and shakes his head. "Be my guest."

Liam goes over and studies the deer. He lifts its head and tries to pull it out of the ditch. After a minute of straining, he stops. "I'll get Earl Ed and Michael to come back and help me load 'em. We can process him the same day we kill Myrtle."

I sigh and palm the back of my neck. My brother is by

far the biggest redneck I know. I'll blame it on him going to Auburn.

Liam and the girls get back in his truck, and he heads toward G-Maw's house. We get in through the passenger door and drive to my parents' house at an insanely slow rate.

"Will it not go any faster than this?"

Collins shakes his head. "That's all me. I'm barely pressing the pedal. That deer shook me up something fierce."

I stare ahead at the road in front of us. The man can drive in downtown Atlanta like it's nothing, and one deer shakes him up? I bite my bottom lip to keep from laughing.

Three times longer than it should've taken us, we pull up to Mama's house. Collins parks near the garage and cuts the engine. I open the door, and we both climb out. I notice that for the first time, he not only leaves his car unlocked but also leaves the keys inside. Maybe he's hoping someone will steal it so he can collect full insurance. That would be my angle.

He goes to the driver's side and examines the damage closely. "That's going to cost me a pretty penny."

I press my lips together. I feel bad for him. He hasn't had the Land Rover all that long, and was so proud of being able to buy it.

I go over and wrap my arm around his waist. "Why don't we both just go to bed? I bet some sleep will do us good after tonight."

"Agreed." He loops an arm around my shoulder, then flinches. "I think I hit my arm on the door."

"Aw." I lean my head against him. Poor guy can't catch a break.

We climb the front steps carefully and go inside. The Christmas lights and warm air calm me almost immediately. I walk with Collins to the basement door. "I hope you're able to get some good rest tonight. Sleep as long as you want tomorrow."

He smiles and pulls me in for a hug. I rest my head on his chest for a few minutes, then lift my head and give him a kiss. He kisses me back, then runs his hand over my hair. "For what it's worth, I actually enjoyed tonight. Right up until the wreck, that is."

I let out a tired laugh. "Me too."

He kisses the tip of my nose and opens the door to the basement. I blow him a kiss as he shuts the door behind him. Then I take just enough time to brush my teeth and change into pajamas before falling into my own bed.

Collins

I TAKE my time walking down the basement stairs. With all the injuries I've endured the past few days, I don't want to chance breaking a leg. I wasn't lying when I told Lacie that I enjoyed tonight. I did.

Sure, some of her family is a little out there. But I've always wanted to be part of a big family. Until that stupid deer mangled my ride, we were having a good time.

I reach the basement floor and flip on the bigger light. My heart sinks when I spot Bully on the edge of my mattress. Out of instinct, I start toward him. I want nothing more than to jerk him down to the ground. Then I remember my butt. I rub the back of my pants and flare my nostrils. Ugh. I can't physically beat this dog. I have to outsmart him.

Food. All dogs love food. Heck, all living things like food. I go to the kitchenette area and open the cabinet where Mrs. Sanderson stocked snacks. There's nothing bacon-flavored, so I go for the next best thing a dog might enjoy—

cheese. I open a bag of Doritos and set them on the corner of the couch. If Bully won't sleep on the floor on a blanket, he may sleep on the couch with Doritos.

Bully sits up and lifts his ears. I step away from the couch as he steps down from the mattress. Brilliant. My plan is working.

I inch toward the mattress as Bully nears the couch. I'm almost to it, when Bully bites the bag of Doritos. Now he just needs to lie down and start eating. Then I can lie down and sleep.

But he doesn't. That stupid mutt runs full speed for my mattress with the bag of chips in his mouth. He leaps onto my covers without even spilling one crumb. But he slobbers plenty.

Within a few seconds, he starts slinging the bag around, spilling chips all over my bed. Then he lies on his back in the middle of the covers and kicks before starting to lick up all the pieces surrounding him.

I slap my face in surrender. It looks like I'll be the one sleeping on the couch. Which isn't so much a couch as it is a loveseat. Oh, and it has no pillow or covers. I debate running to the mattress and grabbing a pillow, but decide I'd rather live instead.

I pick up the blanket folded in the corner, which was meant for Bully. Unfolded, it comes to my knees. I sigh. This must be Bully's actual blanket. With no other options, I settle for rummaging through the closet beside the bathroom until I find an older throw pillow and a spare blanket. It's a pink comforter with Disney princesses on the front, but it looks warm and soft, so who cares? Better than a solid color soiled by Doritos and dog breath.

I brush my teeth, go to the bathroom, and change into my pajamas. When I come back into the main room, Bully is on his back, snoring loudly. I shake my head and snatch the throw pillow from the ground, positioning it at the end of the loveseat and getting my princess cover ready.

I turn off the overhead light and squeeze onto the short couch. This is not intended for six-foot men to sleep on. But it's either here, the concrete floor, or share a bed with the beast. So I make the best of it by scrunching up my legs and covering my head with the pink throw to try and muffle the sound of Bully's snoring.

So much for getting some rest.

As I lie in the dark with the moon casting shadows across dozens of dead animals, while trying to ignore the sounds of the one live animal in the room, all I can think about is Lacie. I love that woman more than life itself. If I didn't, I'd crawl back to my beat-up Land Rover and head for the highway.

CHAPTER ELEVEN

Lacie

I wake and check my phone. It's a little before seven, and I feel well rested. I sit up and stretch my arms toward the ceiling. It's Christmas Eve, and my first holiday with Collins. Even more fun, it's going to start snowing soon.

I get dressed and go to the bathroom to brush my teeth and do my makeup. It's nice not having to fight Liam for the bathroom. This early in the morning, he's either sound asleep or hunting.

I pull half of my hair back in a barrette and practically skip toward the living room. Christmas Eve is my favorite day. Something about the anticipation of Christmas morning and the candlelight service at church makes it all so magical. For a brief time, Wisteria is less *Hart of Dixie* and more Hallmark. The way most outsiders romanticize a small town.

Speaking of Hallmark, Mama is curled up on the couch

with the John Deere blanket, dabbing the corners of her eyes. As soon as I spot Rob Lowe on the TV, I know what's up. I drop my shoulders and step up behind the couch. "Mama, I told you not to watch *The Christmas Shoes*. You can't handle it."

Mama sniffles and turns to face me. "But it's just so good, sweetie."

"So are Oreos, but if we ate those as much as you watch this movie each year, we'd all be borrowing pants from Earl Ed."

Mama twists back around and pauses the TV. "I guess you're right. I'll put in *Elf*." She gets up and puts the movie in the DVD player, then curls back under her blanket.

A giddy laugh escapes me. *Elf* is my favorite Christmas movie. After watching it for the first time as a little girl, I tried to use syrup whenever we ate spaghetti. Then Daddy let me one time when Mama was gone on a church trip. That was all it took for me to realize that recipe was better suited for the North Pole. But Daddy made me eat the whole plate just to get it out of my system. To this day, I don't eat spaghetti.

I circle the couch and sit by Mama. Not long after the opening credits finish, we hear a faint beep.

"Robin, the oven," Daddy yells from the kitchen. We no longer trust him to check the oven thanks to the biscuit disaster of 2012.

Mama tosses the blanket over to me and hurries to the kitchen. I lie back against the cushions and watch as Elf discovers he's really human.

"Lacie, we have monkey bread."

That announcement is all it takes for me to forget about *Elf* and head toward the kitchen. I pour a glass of milk, then smell something woodsy behind me. Not good woodsy like cologne, but the kind of woodsy that lets you know someone's been camping or riding four-wheelers way too long. I turn to see Liam standing behind me.

"Can you pour me a glass?"

I want to put the milk back and tell him to take a shower, but it's Christmas, so I nod. "Get a cup."

He hands me a plastic cup with a faded picture of Dale Earnhardt Jr. on the side. I fill it and hand it back.

"Thanks." He halfway grins at me. It must be a Christmas miracle.

Liam sits at the counter and reaches for the monkey bread. Mama slaps his hand, and I bite back a laugh. "Wash your hands first," she scolds.

He stands and throws back his head as if she's just asked him to enlist in the military instead of use simple hygiene.

"Did you kill anything?" Daddy peeks over his paper toward Liam. He's been reading that same paper for three days. It can't be that interesting. I think it's all a ruse to get out of watching movies with Mama.

"No, sir. I guess all the deer know it's a holiday." Liam laughs at his own joke. The rest of us stay silent and go about fixing our plates. Of course, Daddy had a plate made before I could even make it in the kitchen.

I pull off some pieces and wait for them to cool down. Mama joins Daddy and me at the table with a cup of coffee. Liam sits by himself at the island, probably so he can hog the rest of the bread. We talk a little about tonight, but we mostly eat in silence.

Then Collins walks in, causing us all to stop and stare. His short hair stands on ends, his eyes are bloodshot, and his shoulders are slumped. I push back my chair and rush over to him.

"What happened? Are you okay?" I've been asking him that a lot lately.

He shrugs. "I didn't get any sleep, but I'll be fine."

"Was the bed not okay?" Mama calls from across the kitchen. "You need some coffee and sugar." She moves to the counter and starts pouring a cup of coffee.

"I slept on the couch."

"You mean that little half-couch?" Even Liam sounds concerned now.

Collins yawns and nods. Mama hands him a Santa mug filled with coffee. "I'll get you some monkey bread."

He lifts the corners of his mouth to form a sloth-like smile. "Thank you." Then he looks at Liam. "Yeah, that little couch. I couldn't get Bully to share the mattress."

Mama scoffs, then narrows her eyes toward Daddy. "Joey, I knew keeping him in here was a bad idea."

Daddy shakes his head. "What? Had you rather be responsible for a litter of mutts in a few months?"

Mama crosses her arms and shakes her head. "I'm so sorry, Collins." She comes over and takes his arm, leading him to the table as if he's old and feeble. Then she piles a bunch of monkey bread on a plate and sets it in front of him.

Liam frowns at the pan that only has two pieces left. He must have a change of heart when he looks at Collins, because he says, "I'll go get Bully off the bed."

I go over and kiss Collins on the head, then start out of the kitchen. "I'll go down and make sure he hasn't destroyed anything of Collins's."

On my way to the basement, I hear Daddy call out, "That dog isn't as bad as y'all think."

Whatever, Daddy.

I follow Liam downstairs to the scene of the crime. Bully is lying in the center of the bed with a bag of Doritos ripped apart. Crumbs are strewn all around the mangled covers. "Oh my."

"Bully," Liam calls. The dog doesn't budge. Liam calls his

name louder. This time, he responds by rolling over on his stomach and letting out a huge fart.

"Ugh." I fan the air in front of my face, which only makes it worse.

Liam laughs and calls up the stairs, "Hey, y'all got to come see this."

Mama and Daddy come down a minute later, shortly followed by a sluggish Collins. Liam points to Bully and laughs. Mama puts her hands on her hips and scowls at Daddy.

"Well, I didn't expect him to do that." We all frown at Daddy after his response. Even Liam.

I look over my shoulder at the couch, which has my old princess cover folded at the end. "Collins, why didn't you come upstairs and sleep on the big couch or recliner?"

He shrugs. "I didn't want to impose on anyone."

My heart melts a little at how considerate he is. Then it aches when I think about how tired he must be. "Liam, why don't you let Collins stay in your room?"

"I'm not sharing my bed."

I roll my eyes. "I mean you sleep down here."

"You know I don't like sleeping in basements."

"Fine. Collins can sleep in my room."

"No, ma'am. I will not have that in my house."

I step in front of Daddy. "That's not what I meant. I will sleep down here."

Daddy blinks. "Well, yes, that's acceptable."

"I'm pretty sure I can make Bully at least sleep on the couch. He minds me."

Collins scratches his head, and his cheeks redden. I didn't mean to insult him, but I also can't help that this dog won't do anything he commands.

Mama goes to the mattress and pats Bully on the leg. He snorts, then sits up. "Move, Bully." She gently tugs the sheet under him until he hops off the mattress. Then she pinches the end of the Doritos bag and moves it to the floor, and rolls up the soiled bedding. "Lacie, I'll put these in the wash."

I nod. Bully wags past us and jumps onto the couch. He scratches at the princess cover and lies on it. We all watch him for a minute before starting back upstairs. On the way up, Daddy's phone rings. He answers it.

"Hey. No, I've been in the basement, so I just now got service." Daddy moves toward the living room window, where we get the best cell service.

Mama retreats to the laundry room, and the rest of us head back to the kitchen. We resume eating now that the Bully situation is hopefully under control.

Daddy steps in a few minutes later. "That was Pop on the phone. They're coming here around lunch."

"I thought they were coming by tomorrow before their trip?" Liam talks with a mouth full of food, but we somehow understand him.

"They decided to leave early. Something about winter weather advisories. Anyway, Nannie is afraid if they wait until tomorrow night, they can't drive to Branson."

I raise an eyebrow at Collins. "Winter weather advisory, imagine that."

Collins smirks. "Yeah, on the way to Missouri."

I twist my mouth and shrug. "We'll see."

I sip my milk and stare out the kitchen window. The sky is almost overcast and it's not even noon. Just like I predicted.

Collins

I SPEND the next few hours on the couch with Lacie. The actual, adult-sized couch upstairs, not the princess-cover one in the basement. Which is now marked by Bully like the mattress.

Not long after Mr. Sanderson and Liam left to buy some salt for the hog, I dozed off next to Lacie. She'd called out for them to not forget milk and bread. I'm not sure if she was being sarcastic or serious, since she's been on a snow kick recently.

I don't know how long I slept, but it wasn't long enough. After some time, I wake up to the sound of the TV. Blinking my eyes open to an old man standing over me, I flinch and sit up.

"Didn't mean to scare you, son." He walks around the front of the couch and extends his hand. "Joseph Sanderson, but you can call me Pop. Everyone else under sixty does."

I shake his hand. "Nice to meet you, Pop. I'm Collins."

"I figured as much." He jerks his thumb toward the front door. "The rest of them are out looking at that hog." He laughs. "Ugly ole gal."

I nod in agreement. "But I'm sure she'll feed many."

He laughs again and eases back onto the couch. He's wearing a Bama cap and a crimson jacket. It's the old, crinkly material my parents refer to as a windbreaker. He removes his cap and runs a hand across his balding head, smoothing out the few stray hairs on top.

"So, Collins, what line of work you in, son?"

"I'm a doctor."

"Oh, well." His eyes bug. "Good for you, what kind?"

"General surgeon."

He laughs and slaps me on the knee. "Good for you. I always knew Lacie would do well." He removes his hand from my knee and stares at the floor. "That Liam. Lord knows who he'll end up with."

"He's still young. I'm sure he'll be fine."

Pop wavers his head. "Maybe so. I dated my share of floozies before settling on Remmie."

I scratch my jaw, unsure of how to respond or whether I should respond at all. Lucky for me, he keeps talking, so I don't have to.

"We met at college."

"Which one?"

"UA." He taps the faded "A" on his jacket. "She was a student, and I was working as a groundskeeper."

I nod.

"I worked that job up until two years ago, when I retired."

"Wow."

"Yep. Worked my way up to mowing the grass on the football field. Got to see Coach Saban every day." He grins at me. I smile back to pretend I'm impressed. "You know, he's shorter than you'd think from seeing him on TV."

"I bet." I stare ahead at the TV, not sure where this is going.

Pop sighs and leans his head back against the couch. We sit in silence until it gets awkward. I'd rather hear him ramble about Nick Saban than deal with silence.

"So you're headed for Branson?"

He exhales. "Yeah. After we both retired, Remmie bought a timeshare there. I told her it was the worst decision she's ever made, aside from marrying me."

I turn toward him with a blank expression. I can't tell if he's joking or serious. His eyebrows are too bushy for me to read his eyes. I wish I'd asked something else about Saban.

"So you just travel now?"

Pop shakes his head. "After about a year of me sitting around the house, we bought a business. But we have to visit Branson three times a year for that timeshare."

I nod. "What kind of business?" Maybe I can eventually steer his away from the timeshare.

"Pawn shop." He gets in my face and whispers, "You know, if you ever need a ring for my granddaughter, we get plenty in every week." He winks, then leans back against the couch.

"Thank you, Pop, that's every generous." I look back at the TV. I already have the perfect ring. I just need the right time to propose.

My stomach twitches when I realize it's Christmas Eve. I'd originally planned to propose on Christmas Eve night. I glance at my watch. It's almost noon. That gives me mere hours to talk to the Sandersons and come up with a plan to ask Lacie. I guess I'll ask her somewhere around here, since Wisteria isn't the quaint little town with a gazebo like I'd pictured in my mind. Besides, Mrs. Sanderson's overkill decorations make a better backdrop than the AstroTurf porch at her grandma's house.

I sigh and lean my head back on the couch as well.

"Sorry, son. I didn't mean to wake you up."

I turn to Pop and grin. "It's fine, really. I didn't sleep well last night is all."

"All the noise in the country get to you?"

I blink. "Actually, I was looking forward to that. I use a sound machine in Atlanta. But I couldn't hear any birds or anything, because Bully snored the whole time."

Pop slaps the couch between us and laughs. It catches me off guard, and I jerk my head up. "That dog is something else. I can't believe Robin let him in this house."

"She didn't want to, which is how he ended up in the basement with me."

"Well, I'll say. Had I known that, I'd have let you stay with us in Tuscaloosa."

I press my lips together and try to imagine what Pop's

house might look like. Is it covered in football memorabilia? Does he decorate it with items from the pawn shop? Before I have to form any kind of response, the front door opens.

Everyone files in, chatting. An older woman who has to be Remmie/Nannie comes to the back of the couch. "Collins, so nice to meet you. I hope Joseph hasn't talked your ear off."

"No, ma'am, he's been pleasant company."

"Good to hear." She turns to Liam and smiles. "Sweetie, go to my car and fetch that Crockpot."

"Yes, ma'am." Liam drops his head and goes outside.

"I made a big pot of corn chowder for lunch."

Liam returns with a crimson Crockpot that has "Roll Tide" printed across the front. "Do you want the other stuff, too?"

"Yes, dear, thanks."

Liam hands her the Crockpot, then jogs out and comes back with several plastic containers. Pop stands and pats his belly, then puts his cap back on his head. I stand and follow everyone into the kitchen.

Mrs. Sanderson plugs in the Crockpot and starts opening containers. We have cornbread, dinner rolls, and some kind of dessert. I know it's Christmas, but I've never seen so many desserts in one week in my life.

"Lacie, grab some bowls for us," Mrs. Sanderson says.

Lacie goes to the cabinet and gets down some bowls, the sets them beside her mom. Mrs. Sanderson ladles out bowls of soup while Pop and Mr. Sanderson sit at the table. When they lean back and stare out the window, I notice their resemblance more. Pop is a grayer, heavier version of his son.

Lacie brings the bowls of soup to the table. Mrs. Sanderson follows her with spoons, and Nannie brings over the breads. I take a seat across from Pop, and Lacie sits beside me.

Everyone glances around the room, and Mrs. Sanderson asks, "Where's Liam?"

Liam walks in, announcing, "I went to wash my hands." He plops down at the end of the table and props his arm over the back of the chair.

Mr. Sanderson says a quick prayer, and then everyone begins eating. It's been a while since I've had corn chowder. Nannie's is much better than the hospital cafeteria's. Hers isn't quite as bland.

We eat and talk for the next hour. I start keeping count of how many times Pop mentions Nick Saban. I lose interest at thirty-three and let my mind wander. I watch Lacie sip her water from a straw and daydream about kissing her, right here, right now. That leads to thoughts of eloping again, but I know she's always wanted a wedding.

That's why no matter what else happens, I have to propose tonight, and I have to make it perfect for her.

CHAPTER TWELVE

Collins

Everyone walks out onto the porch to wave goodbye to Nannie and Pop. They climb into a crimson-and-white van with "Roll Tide" painted down the side. So that's a little extreme. Perhaps if I'd been awake to see them arrive, I'd have been better prepared for all the Saban stories.

Pop waves out the window and honks the horn, which plays part of the Alabama fight song. Everyone waves back, then we go inside. I just thought I knew extreme football fans until I met Pop.

Once we're all in the living room, Mrs. Sanderson announces, "I'm going to help with the Angel Tree. Lacie would you like to come?"

Lacie nods toward me. "I don't want to leave Collins by himself. I think I'll stay here this year."

Before I can think, I say, "I'll go help, too." Not that I want to go anywhere but back to napping. However, the last thing I want to do is mess up any plans Lacie had made before I crashed her family Christmas.

"Really?" She squints at me.

"Yeah." I nod and smile as if I can't wait to go do whatever helping with the Angel Tree entails.

"Great, we can use the extra strength." Mrs. Sanderson smiles at me.

"Well, I think I'll go help Liam find a deer." Mr. Sanderson claps his hands together and looks at his son. "I don't really want to end up eating meat off that one you boys pulled out of the ditch last night."

Liam makes a mischievous face. "Can I at least mount it?"

Mr. Sanderson folds his arms and looks down at him. "Son, it's a disgrace to all hunters to mount an animal you didn't kill."

"Fine." Liam slumps his shoulders and sighs.

He stomps toward his room like an upset toddler. Mr. Sanderson goes off in the opposite direction.

"Let me grab my purse, and we'll go," Mrs. Sanderson says.

Lacie and I lean against the back of the couch while her mom goes to the other end of the house and returns with her purse. We follow her to her car.

We drive past Waffle House and into town. She turns at Dollar General and goes down a narrow street. At the end is a tall building. The front sign reads, "Wisteria City Hall." A good many cars are already parked around the building. She parks to the side, and we get out.

We walk around to the front, and I open the door for them. The lobby area is decorated with poinsettias and black-and-white photos. I study a few of the photos as we walk past. They are old photos from around town.

We enter a larger area where people are bustling around

with toys and boxes and clipboards. An older man who looks to be in charge comes up to us. It's like we're in Santa's workshop, except Santa is wearing overalls.

"Hi, Robin. Lacie. And who do we have here?" He adjusts his glasses and looks me over.

"I'm Collins."

"Nice to have you. I'm Brother Billy, pastor of Wisteria Worship Center." He extends his hand, and I shake it. "We appreciate your help."

"My pleasure." I feign a grin. *My pleasure?* What am I, a Chick-fil-A drive-thru attendant?

He turns his attention back to Mrs. Sanderson. "Robin, I need you making calls about the deliveries like usual."

"Okay."

"Lacie, you and Collins can go over to Annette and see where she needs you."

"Will do." Lacie smiles, then loops her arm through mine. Mrs. Sanderson heads back toward the lobby, while Billy greets the next people coming in.

I take in all the action as Lacie leads me across the massive space. "There's a lot of people here."

"Yep. For all its pitfalls, Wisteria is actually pretty great about helping neighbors in need."

We stop at a table filled with boxes. Standing in front of it is a tall, slim redhead chatting with someone and holding a clipboard. As soon as she turns around, she smiles and hugs Lacie. "Lacie. So good to see you here."

"It's nice to see you, too." Lacie smiles and points to me. "This is my boyfriend, Collins. We're here for whatever you need."

"Perfect. First thing I need is for you to check over some of the information we're getting in from the call room."

"Okay."

After Lacie agrees, Annette leads us over to another table

stacked with papers. She points out some folders and starts talking about sorting out children based on address then ages. She seems to have a well-oiled system, with color-coded labels and everything. I lean forward to get a closer look at the call sheets she's pointing out, when my stomach rumbles.

I step back a few inches so Annette and Lacie don't hear the dinosaurs fighting inside my gut. I try and listen to the instructions, but my insides are waging war. I grip my belt and adjust my pants to try and alleviate some of the pain.

When Annette stops talking and walks away, I join Lacie behind the table and stare at the stack of papers.

"Why don't you start sorting by age? Then I'll go through and find the streets close together," she says.

"Okay." I loosen my belt buckle under the table to ease my stomach pain. That, along with simply sitting, seems to help.

I'm making my way through a huge stack of papers, feeling pretty accomplished, when a lady brings another stack to me. "I just got a new note that we need to add a few phone numbers to these."

"Yes, ma'am."

"If you can add these when I call them out, it will be quicker for us all."

I grab a pen from between Lacie and me. She reads the first name from her clipboard, and I find that page. "4555."

I wait. Then she repeats the same numbers. "Is that all?"

She tilts her head as if she's not sure what I'm asking. Lacie twists toward me in her chair and laughs. "She means 787-4555."

"What?"

"Just write it out, Collins."

I do as Lacie advises. The woman scrunches her nose at us in confusion. Lacie looks up and grins. "He's not from around here."

"Oh." The woman continues on with the next few sheets, this time emphasizing "787" before each one. She sighs after she's done. Did spouting out three extra numbers each time really take so much extra energy? She turns on her heels and heads back to where she came from.

Lacie bursts out laughing.

"What?"

She continues to laugh. "I'm sorry. It's just funny you didn't know."

"Didn't know what?"

She fans her face and catches her breath. "Every landline in Wisteria begins with 787."

"For real?"

Lacie nods. She laughs again, and I can't help but join her. From the way she throws back her head to her dark eyes dancing with joy, her laughter is contagious.

But then my stomach lets out a trumpet blast.

"Whoa." Lacie's eyes widen. "Are you okay?"

"Where's the restroom? I think it may be Nannie's corn chowder."

Lacie fights off another laugh and points toward the side exit.

"Thanks." I stand, forgetting that my belt is unbuckled and dangling on my pants. I rush out the side door and find the restrooms down a long hallway.

The men's restroom has a sign on the door that reads, "Closed for cleaning." I knock on the door, but nobody answers, and it's locked. I debate going back in the main room and asking if there's another restroom. Surely, in a building this size there has to be.

My stomach turns another somersault, refusing to let me find another alternative. Against my better judgement, I pull open the door to the women's bathroom and bolt inside. Luckily, nobody is in there. Well, except for a pair of high heels beneath one stall. I ignore whomever she is and open the next door.

At last, I can put my stomach out of its misery.

I try and wait until I don't hear anyone else in the bathroom before I sneak out to wash my hands and make my exit. Several people come and go while I'm in there, and I imagine Lacie laughing more and more with every minute that passes. I can't let her know I ended up in the women's restroom. She will already never let me live this down.

When I hear nothing but silence, I leave my hiding spot and wash my hands. Then I make sure my belt is properly buckled and open the door.

I come face to face with a teenage girl. She shrieks and runs off in the opposite direction.

"I'm not . . . wait . . . it's not." I give up trying to explain when she disappears out another exit. Great, just what I need.

I slink back toward the main room. With every step, I pray I never see that girl again. Making it back to our table without her in sight, I sigh and take my seat beside Lacie.

She looks up from putting papers in a blue folder. "Everything come out okay?" She bats her eyelashes and smiles.

"Haha." I pick up a handful of papers and stack them neatly before separating the pages. We work side by side for a few minutes. Lacie teases me about my stomach, and I joke that her stomach wouldn't be so strong if she didn't filter a gallon of Starbucks though it every day.

She pouts, then I pull her close and kiss her cheek. We both laugh.

"There!" I look up to see who yelled. The girl who saw me coming out of the restroom is pointing at my face. She steps toward us, with none other than Bradley by her side. "This guy, sheriff. He was the one in the women's bathroom."

Bradley twists his jaw and crosses his arms, as if trying to make sense of this. I catch Lacie's face from the corner of my eye. Her eyes are the size of marbles, and she's no longer laughing.

Oh boy. How will I ever explain this one?

Lacie

COLLINS WAS in the women's restroom? I don't know what to make of this. Marcie wouldn't have any reason to lie, but neither would Collins have a reason to go in the women's restroom. Especially given the condition of his stomach. I shake my head.

"Let me explain." Collins slides up from his slumped position and glances back and forth from me to Bradley. "The men's restroom was closed for cleaning. I knocked and tried to open the door, but it was locked."

"That's for safety reasons. The custodian is a woman," Bradley states matter-of-factly, arms still folded stiffly across his chest.

"See, safety. But this man went in our bathroom." Marcie pouts and points an accusing finger at Collins's nose.

He stares at it, then turns to me and Bradley again. "Look, my stomach was about to explode. I've never been in this building until today. If I had even a minute to go find another restroom, or run down the street to Dollar General, or even behind a tree, I would have. But I was desperate."

Bradley nods. "I believe you, man. I've been there."

Marcie frowns and shrugs. "Do you know this guy, Lacie?"

I lace my arm through Collins's and rest my hand on his bicep. "He's been my boyfriend for a year. He's a doctor and a good person. Harmless, really."

Bradley nods. "He's pretty harmless, I'd say."

Collins exhales and gives me a disgusted face. I pat his arm in an attempt to thwart Bradley's comment.

Marcie turns her attention to me, then back to Bradley. "If you both say so."

We nod at her, and Collins grins. Her lips curve up at last. She picks at the end of her sweater and shrugs. "Sorry about this. But you did really scare me."

"I'm sorry, too. It was never my intention." Collins nods. "To scare you or to go into the women's restroom."

"Thanks." She turns her back to us and speed walks toward the toy section. We all instinctively look her way, but she avoids eye contact. Probably for the best.

Bradley sits on the edge of our table. I scoot my chair closer to Collins so his butt isn't in my view. "Dude, sorry about that."

Collins slaps his hand on the table. "Hey, I'm glad she was being safe."

"Yeah, but I know that's gotta stink to get caught coming out of there." Bradley punches Collin's arm and grins. "No pun intended about the stink."

Collins runs a hand down his face and exhales. "It wasn't my proudest moment."

Bradley twists around to me. "What'd you feed the man, Enchilada?"

I shake my head. "Nannie's corn chowder."

Bradley clinches his teeth and turns back to Collins. "Oof, dude. That's rough on anyone the first time. But you kinda build an immunity after a few rounds."

Collins sits like a statue, staring at the floor in front of our table. I pick up a folder and get back to work. Maybe if I ignore Bradley, he'll leave.

"Hey, why don't you two come help me deliver the first batch of gifts?"

I set down the paper in my hand and look at Collins. He's still staring at the floor. "Thanks, Bradley, but we've got a lot more papers to sort."

Collins asks in a monotone voice, "Will that girl be there?"

"No. Just us and a bunch of toys," Bradley answers.

Collins pushes back his chair and stands. He looks at Bradley. "I'm in."

"That's the Christmas spirit, Collins." Bradley slaps him on the back.

I choke back a scream and stand as well. "Let me tell Annette she'll need to fill this spot."

"No worries, I'll go tell her you guys got promoted." Bradley pats Collins and me on the shoulders this time, then darts off to find Annette.

I close my eyes and wish I could open them to an alternate reality. Nope. I'm still in the civic center with Collins, and now Bradley and Annette are headed our way.

"I think it's great you guys will help Bradley. That will shave off some time. I can get some of the older people to file papers."

I muster a fake smile. It's not Annette's fault I'm caught in this weird Collins-Bradley web like some girl in a vampire novel.

Annette starts motioning toward a group of older ladies. We follow Bradley out the back door to the parking lot, and he leads us to his old Chevy.

"Do you want to take my mama's car?" I don't care for Bradley's driving or his truck.

"That's so sweet of you to offer, but we need the truck to

hold all this stuff." He pats the bed of the truck. I crane my neck to see that it's filled with boxes.

"Where are we going?" Collins asks.

"A children's home near the end of town. They've got like ten kids right now."

Bradley opens his door. As soon as Collins opens the passenger door for us, Bradley starts assigning seats. "Sorry it's a single cab. I guess it's best if Lacie sits in the middle. Since she's the smallest and all."

Naturally, he'd think it's best I sit there. It's the tractor and parade ride all over again. I grit my teeth and climb inside. Collins gets in behind me and slams the door.

I squeeze my knees together and hug my thighs against Collins's leg. I want them far as possible from the gear stick before Bradley starts driving. I would hate for him to "accidentally" graze my leg as he changes gears.

He barrels out of the parking lot, totally disregarding the dozen or so boxes in the bed of the truck. With the way the wind is whipping, our only chance at not losing one is how tightly they're packed.

We drive toward the edge of town, mostly in silence. Bradley has the radio on, which helps muffle the sounds of the old truck. It's a country station, but all the songs they play are Christmas. That brings me some relief on this unwanted ride.

He turns down a dirt road, causing me to grip the dash. Collins wraps a hand around my waist to help hold me back. My seat belt is merely a dry-rotted lap band that doesn't do the job.

At the end of the dirt road, there's a large farmhouse with a cedar tree decorated in colored lights. Bradley parks near the edge of the yard behind a barn.

"Why are we parked so far back?" I ask.

"I gotta get ready." Bradley gets out and opens his tool-box. He comes back with a Santa suit.

I laugh. "Seriously?"

"Well, yeah, unless . . ." He holds the Santa suit out and nods at Collins.

"I don't know." Collins shakes his head. "You've probably done this before."

"Yeah, but you're a little shorter and heavier than me. It will look more authentic."

Collins frowns at Bradley. I put my hand on his knee. "You don't have to do this."

Bradley laughs and switches his cowboy hat for a Santa hat. "Yeah, I'm probably better with kids anyway, being a sheriff and all."

Collins's eyes narrow. He doesn't like it when anyone makes the assumption he can't do something. That's one of the qualities I love most about him. "Hand me the suit." Collins reaches across me and jerks the suit from Bradley's hand.

"All right, big dog, it's yours." Bradley tosses the hat back in the truck and puts his own hat back on.

Collins opens our door and pulls the Santa suit over his own clothes. He buttons it up, then puts on the beard and wig. I get out and adjust the frizzy gray beard over his own trim brown beard and put the hat on his head. "There." I smile, then kiss him gently on the lips.

"Come on, you two. You're gonna confuse the kids."

"There's no kids back here," I bark back at Bradley. Collins winks at me, then takes my hand. We get back in the truck and drive the short distance to the front of the farmhouse.

Bradley parks, and we all start unloading gifts. It doesn't take but a few minutes for a kid to spot us out the window. Kids from toddlers to young teens run down the large front porch. A woman who looks about mid-thirties follows behind with a baby.

"Santa, nice to see you." She smiles at us as the younger kids hug Collins's legs.

"Ho, ho ho. I have gifts. Why don't you all go to the porch while my elves and I unload them?"

Bradley rolls his eyes and mouths "elves." I elbow him in the ribs and open the tailgate. The three of us start unloading boxes as the woman herds the kids to the porch. After two trips, we have everything to the front door.

"Thank you all so much." The woman smiles as she shifts the baby to one hip and props the door open for us.

"You're welcome. You have a lovely home," I say.

"Oh, thank you. I'm Lina." She extends a slim hand.

I shake it and smile. "Lacie."

The guys push the boxes inside the door as Lina and I gather the kids around the fireplace. Collins sits in a nearby recliner and resumes his Santa laugh. "Now, if Elf Bradley will be so kind as to bring me a gift, I'll start rewarding you good boys and girls."

My heart warms at the excitement on all the kids' faces. Even the older ones are delighted to see Santa. It's a shame how spoiled the rest of us are. When we were nine and four-teen, Mama had to bribe Liam and me to get one last photo with Santa in the Tuscaloosa mall. We only did it so we could go eat Japanese and get ice cream. Shame washes over me at how selfish we were, and still are to some degree.

Bradley calls out a name, and a young boy with missing front teeth runs and jumps in Collins's lap. Collins lets out a breathy Santa laugh and rocks back in the chair. Bradley hands him the box and Collins grins at the boy. "Do you think your front teeth are in here?"

The boy shrugs. Collins holds up the box, and the kid rips off the paper. It's a hoverboard. The boy screams and hugs Collins. He rubs the kid's back and lets out another "ho, ho, ho."

Next is an older girl who stands beside Collins and smiles shyly. She gets her own makeup set and some jewelry. Every gift is special to each individual child, and rather expensive, too. I choke back a tear as these kids marvel at their gifts. Lina stands beside me sniffling, wiping away crocodile tears.

"How long have they been here?"

She sniffs again before answering. "Some are siblings. They've been here six months, which is longer than the others. Kids come and go here. My husband and I started fostering five years ago when we found out I can't have kids."

My jaw drops. "I'm so sorry."

She shakes her head. "It's fine. We bought and fixed up this big place with plans to have a huge family. But God had other plans." She smiles at me through her tears and hugs the baby close.

My heart flutters in my chest as I watch her interact with the baby who isn't even hers. Then the last little girl climbs on Collins's lap. He smiles at me, and I return the smile. I can't wait to have a family with him one day.

"Santa, I have you a gift, too."

"Oh, ho, ho, you do?" Collins rocks the little girl as she grins. She holds a shoe box up to his face and opens it.

A tiny kitten pops its head out of the box. Awww. I can't take any more sweetness. It's like I'm living out a TV Christmas special. I'm half expecting Lina to confess she's an angel in disguise.

But Collins doesn't share my excitement. At least, not about the kitten. He rears his head back and sneezes so big that his fake beard falls off on one side. The little girl screams, jumps down, and tosses the box. The cat flies up and clings to Collins's chest. He tries to shake it loose, but its claws are stuck.

Collins wiggles in the recliner, leaning farther back until the legs pop up and it falls over. The cat hisses, and when they hit the floor with a thud, it runs off. I guess the impact loosened its grip on his felt suit. Collins lies on the floor, his feet in the air. All the kids are either screaming, laughing, or crying.

I cover my face. So much for living out a Christmas movie. Maybe *The Nightmare Before Christmas*. I peek through my fingers to see Bradley cackling as he tries to flip the recliner back into place.

I apologize to Lina, who offers me a sympathetic smirk. I suspect she's trying not to laugh, too. As quickly as we can, the three of us dart out the door. Thank God, that was the last gift.

We climb in Bradley's truck and hightail it back to town.

CHAPTER THIRTEEN

Collins

I jerk around in the tiny truck, shrugging off the Santa suit as we go. Between my eyes puffing up and watering, I can hardly see. I sneeze, cough, and choke, unable to control my breathing. Lacie pushes her palm up and down my back, massaging me. It helps a little, but not enough.

I cough and sneeze at the same time. Even as a medical professional, I've never witnessed that before. "I need Benadryl."

"Bradley, DG, ASAP!"

"I'm going the top of the speed limit," Bradley snaps back at Lacie.

"You're the sheriff. Drive as fast as you want!"

"I'm in my personal truck, and I need to set a good example."

"If you don't speed—"

"Oh my gosh, will you two quit fighting?"

Lacie wraps her arm around my shoulders. "I'm sorry, babe."

I sigh and sneeze some more. I'm too out of it to tell if Bradley speeds up, but he doesn't say anything else.

"I never knew your cat allergy was this bad." Lacie's voice is warm and comforting. Too bad it can't help me catch my breath.

I respond in between coughs. "Neither did I. I've never touched a cat until now."

"You've never touched a cat?"

I liked it better when Bradley was quiet.

I sneeze again. "Nope. Mom always scared me out of it. She apparently knew the severity of my allergy." I cough and clear my throat. "I took allergy shots until age fifteen."

"You poor baby." Lacie leans her head on me.

Bradley comes to a stop, and I hear the door open. "Go, Lacie, get whatever y'all need."

I rub my eyes and listen as Bradley sits back beside me and shuts the door. I turn my head but can barely see his face. My eyes are almost swollen shut. "How do I look?"

I think he's smiling. If I find out later he is, I'll kill him. But right now, I don't have the strength. I sneeze without covering my mouth. He jerks back, and I take momentary pleasure in that slight revenge.

"Dude, have you ever seen the movie *Hitch*?"

I groan and plop back against the seat of the truck. When I do, my head bumps against the back glass. I rub the back of my head. "Ouch."

"Hey, be glad I don't have a gun sitting back there like usual." This time, Bradley is smiling. I can hear it in his voice.

I go ahead and close my eyes, sending tears down the corners of my cheeks. After a few more coughs, the door opens again. I hear the shuffling of Lacie getting in and Bradley closing the door.

"Here. Take this." Lacie opens my hand and puts some pills in it. After I toss them in my mouth, she shoves a bottle in my hand. I take a sip. It's water. I could probably use something stronger, but my scratchy throat is happy with that.

Bradley cranks the truck and backs out of the parking lot. A minute or two later, he parks again.

"Wait here," Lacie calls out as she gets out of his truck. I sit, helpless as a blind man, squinting my sore eyes. A cool wind hits my side when she opens my door. Lacie takes hold of my hand and helps me down from the truck.

"Come on, we'll go home."

"I'll wait here while you get your mom."

I lean against the seat, the truck door still open. The cold air actually soothes my throbbing face. After what feels like both an eternity and a second, Lacie rushes toward me with Mrs. Sanderson by her side.

"Oh, Collins. Bless your heart. Let's get you home to rest." Mrs. Sanderson loops an arm through mine, and Lacie does the same on my other side. I'm exhausted from all the coughing and wheezing and sneezing, and my vision is still foggy, so I'm more than happy to let them lead me to her car. Lacie opens the back door, and I fall inside. I lie across the seat and close my eyes.

The next thing I remember, Lacie is shaking my side, trying to wake me. I sit up and blink, my vision a little clearer than before. The overdose of Benadryl must be kicking in. My eyes aren't as sore, and I'm sleepy.

Lacie helps me up the porch steps and into her room. I blink at all the bright colors swirling together. It's very much a teenage girl's room. "Go ahead and rest. I moved your things from the basement while you napped earlier."

"Thanks," I creak through my scratchy throat.

I lie back on the bed and sigh heavily. It's only a twin bed, but it's soft and the normal height for a bed. I so prefer this over sleeping a foot off the floor with Bully. I sink my head into the pillow, and Lacie pulls the covers over me.

That's the last thing I remember until I wake up hours later, a face full of Bradley.

It's not real Bradley, thank goodness. Instead, I'm on my side, facing an old prom photo of him hugged up to Lacie. So, yeah, basically almost as bad as real Bradley. A string of curses run through my head, but my throat is still too sore to say them. It's not like it would do any good to cuss at a picture anyway.

I slam it down on the nightstand and push myself off the bed. After a quick glance around to celebrate my regained sense of sight, I cross the room and lean against the dresser. I push aside a pink sash that has "Apple Sauce Queen" written in glitter and check my appearance in the mirror. Face is still red, eyes slightly puffy. But I couldn't pass for Hitch, so that's a relief.

My suitcase, toiletry bag, and Apple Watch are sitting nearby in a neat little stack. Slight panic washes through me at the thought of Lacie moving my things. My suitcase wasn't zipped when I left it before. What if she noticed the pocket at the bottom, and what if she looked in it?

I frantically dive toward my things and toss the toiletry bag to the floor, unzipping the suitcase and moving clothes until I feel the ring box, safe inside the security pocket at the back. I turn and sit against the wall, dropping my head in my hands.

There's no way she saw it. I had that pocket zipped, with everything covering it. Besides, Lacie and I don't keep secrets from one another. Well, except for me hiding the ring. And my momentary omission of going to the women's restroom.

Ugh. Maybe I do keep some things from Lacie. I ball my hands into fists and pound my forehead. Thanks to all the Benadryl, I barely feel it. Then it dawns on me that it's Christmas Eve, when I'd planned to propose, except I have no plan, and I have no idea what time it is. I fumble around for my watch. *Five p.m.!*

I unzip the pocket and take out the ring box, popping it open to stare at it. How can I be so pathetic? I have no plan, and I haven't talked to her parents yet. Even if I did propose and she did say "yes," her mom will want photos. And I look like my face has been stung by bees, or at the very least, endured a bad sunburn.

I raise my head and stare at the ceiling. There, above my head, glow-in-the-dark stars spell out "Lacie N Bradley." Seriously? This must be a sign from the universe. I close my eyes and shut the ring box, gripping it tightly and praying for a sign. Anything at all, besides plastic stars aligning against me.

Then I hear a knock on the door. Before I can fully open my eyes, the door starts to open. I scramble to shove the ring in my pocket as Lacie peeks through.

"Hey, how are you feeling?"

I shrug and try to play it off as if I'm just casually hanging out by an open suitcase in the middle of the floor. Lacie comes inside and sits beside me. I put my hand between us on the floor so she won't feel the ring bulging in my pocket.

I'm tempted to propose right now, right here. But I chicken out. I'm just vain enough to not propose with a red, swollen face. And I'm just superstitious enough to not do it while sitting beneath the words "Lacie N Bradley."

"Have you been up long?"

I shake my head. "Only a few minutes."

"Good, I wanted you to rest. You look better." She smiles and nods enthusiastically.

I do? I can only imagine how rough I looked before my nap.

"We're about to eat dinner, if you're hungry."

"That sounds good." I can always eat, especially now after flushing away all my calories hours ago.

"Okay, well just come out when you're ready." Lacie runs her hand across my hair and kisses me on the cheek.

I give her a sheepish smile and lean my head against the wall. As soon as she leaves the room, I stand up and change shirts. I believe all the cat hair was contained on the Santa suit, but I still don't want to take any chances.

I comb my hair, spritz on some cologne, and gargle some mouthwash. I forget that I'm nowhere near a sink, so I swallow it, sticking my tongue out and coughing as it burns my throat. Well, that's one way to clear up my lungs.

I reach into my pocket to pull out the ring, then change my mind. The clock is ticking. I best keep it with me. Who knows? Maybe I can find a chance during or after dinner to talk to Mr. Sanderson about the proposal.

With a renewed sense of confidence, I step out of the room and shut the door behind me. Before I take my hand off the knob, I open the door and flip on the light, then I shut it and walk away. I don't want to give the "Lacie N Bradley" a chance to shine before I go to bed.

Halfway down the long hallway, I hear voices. I assume it's Lacie's parents until I reach the living room. Then I hear several people laughing and talking. I round the corner and notice at least twenty people hovering around the counter-tops in the kitchen. Lacie finds me and wraps her arm around my waist.

"What is this?" I ask.

"A progressive dinner."

"A what?"

"Progressive dinner."

"Like Progressive Soup?"

Lacie laughs and pats my back. "One house serves appetizers, another the main course, and another dessert."

I wrinkle my forehead and scan the room. A lot of Lacie's family is here, but there are some other people I don't know. Oh, and Bradley.

I shove my hand in my pocket and grip the ring box. I wonder what Lacie would say if I got everyone's attention and asked her to marry me in the middle of the kitchen. Right beside the tractor tree.

Mrs. Sanderson interrupts my train of thought by walking up and shoving a paper plate at my chest. I take it and mutter a "thanks." She motions for us to fall in line behind the people fixing finger foods.

I abandon my ring box to put chicken wings on my plate. It's probably for the best.

Lacie

I LEAD Collins to the piano bench in the corner of the living room. That's the last place people will think to sit, and it'll give us more privacy. I can tell he's still a bit loopy from all that medicine. Once we got home, I checked the back of the bottle. I think I gave him twice the recommended amount out of panic . . . and ignorance.

"Who plays the piano?" he asks as we sit down.

"Nobody in my family."

He glances at the piano and wrinkles his forehead before facing me. "Do you guys do this thing every year?"

"What thing?" I pop a cheese straw in my mouth and

study his face. Even with the redness and slight swelling, I can see his confusion seeping through.

"This progression dinner deal."

I nod and swallow my food. "Yeah, ever since I can remember."

"Huh."

"You've really never heard of one?"

He shakes his head.

I shrug. "Must be a small-town thing." I put the back of my hand to his forehead, then his cheek. "You don't feel as hot as before."

He presses his hand against his face. "Yeah, I feel like the swelling's gone way down." He blinks and moves his eyes around. "And I can see now."

"It's a Christmas miracle." I lift up my hands and giggle. Collins laughs, too.

It's good to hear him laugh for the first time in hours. And not his fake Santa laugh, but his real one.

He chews a bite of cracker and cheeseball, then scans the room. "So, who are all these people? You know, besides your mom's family. Oh, and I remember Jack and that younger guy. They shot with us yesterday."

I nod. "Yeah, that's his cousin, Jonah. He's from Apple Cart but hunts a lot with Liam. They go to Auburn together. The other guy beside them is Tanner. Jack's best friend, who also went to Auburn."

"Okay, and the rest live in Wisteria?"

"Yep." I point to different groups mingling around as I fill Collins in on who everyone is. "That group of women are Mama's Bible study friends. The short, heavyset one is Brother Billy's wife."

"The overalls preacher?"

"That's the one." I laugh. "Those old men in camo are in

the gun club with Uncle Earl. You might recognize that one from Waffle House."

Collins shakes his head. "Sorry, they all look the same to me. Kind of like the men on *Duck Dynasty*."

I tilt my head and try to imagine seeing them all for the first time. "I guess you're right."

Paul walks past us with two Styrofoam plates. He nods his head before going out the front door. I smirk at him and eat another deer-meat sausage ball.

"Did your mom make all this food?"

"Goodness, no. Almost everyone here brought something." Except for Paul. He's no give and all take.

Collins bites into a jalapeño and chews. He widens his eyes and nods. "Mmmm, who brought this?"

I lean closer to get a look at what he's eating. "Probably Jack. That's a deer popper."

"Deer popper?"

"Yeah, this jalapeño deer thing that Jack makes for his hunting lodge."

Collins puts the rest of it in his mouth and nods again. He swallows. "You need to make these when we get back home."

My limbs tingle at the words "we get back home." Even though I know he means when we both get back to Atlanta, I like the idea of sharing a home with Collins. Maybe one day in the near future, we will.

"Remind me to take some deer steaks home, and I will." I grin, and Collins reaches for my hand.

I scoot closer to him and admire the lights on the living room tree. Mama always puts the biggest tree in here. It's covered with all the ornaments Liam and I made over the years from art class, church camps, and every other random childhood event. It also has an ornament from every place we've been over the years. Disney World, the Grand Canyon, the beach. Now that we're twenty-five and twenty, she has no trouble filling the branches. I secretly think she collected so many sentimental ornaments as an excuse for Daddy to get her a massive tree.

Once we finish our food, Collins and I return to throw away our plates and refill our apple cider. Several people stop us along the way to introduce themselves. Others nod or greet him for a second or third time.

I catch Bradley out of the corner of my eye, talking to Uncle Earl and Jonah. I'm glad he isn't nearby. I've had enough of him for one day.

We stand by the kitchen island and talk to Michael and Krystal for a few minutes. She catches me off guard by grabbing my hand and sticking it to her belly. "Feel that?"

"No."

She pushes my hand lower on her belly. This is really awkward now.

"Feel it now?"

"Yes, I do." I hate to lie, especially during Christmas, but if I don't, I'm afraid she'll lower my hand again. I make eye contact with the manger scene in the windowsill and mouth a "sorry."

I hear someone behind us say, "We better head out."

Everyone migrates toward the living room, and people start putting on coats. Those who brought a dish take it out with them. I stay back in the kitchen to put away anything left. Mama scurries around, gathering any cups and plates on the tables and chairs.

Collins plops down on a stool at the kitchen island and yawns. "That was a nice party."

I smile at him. "I'm glad you enjoyed it. Everyone seems to like you."

"They're good people."

"It helped a tiny bit that Aunt Misty wasn't here."

"Lacie." Mama swats my arm on her way to the trash can.

"What?"

She gives me her "I raised you better than that" face.

"Do you ladies need any help with anything?" Collins asks.

"No, we'll do a deep clean later. We just take out all the trash before going to the next house."

"Next house?"

I stop in front of the refrigerator door and turn to Mama. She freezes from bagging the trash and meets my gaze. I look at Collins. "Yeah, for the main course, remember?"

His forehead wrinkles. "But you already hosted the appetizers here."

"Yeah, then the next house is the main course."

"So, then why . . . Oh . . ." His eyes widen at the realization that we're not only hosting the appetizers, but participating in the other courses as well.

My stomach sinks when his face morphs from relaxed to perplexed. And just when he was fitting in so nicely.

CHAPTER FOURTEEN

Collins

"Let me grab my coat." I try to not let my frustration come through in my voice. But the last thing I want is to hop around Wisteria, eating all night.

I was perfectly content with the deer poppers and hot wings we had here. And the only time I spoke to Mr. Sanderson was when he was surrounded by old men drinking coffee. Not exactly the right setting to strike up a conversation about my intentions with his daughter.

I open Lacie's bedroom door and bend down for my coat. I go ahead and grab my keys, too. When I straighten, she's standing behind me. "Ready?"

"Yeah." I force a stiff smile and shrug on my coat. She reaches for the light switch and I shake my head at her. "Don't turn that off."

"Why?" Her eyebrows pinch together in confusion.

I sigh and point above my head. Her eyes follow my finger, and she blushes. "Sorry, I forgot all about that."

"It's fine, I just don't want to be greeted with it when I come home."

She walks up to me. "Put me on your shoulders."

"What?" Now I'm the one confused.

"Just do it." She pulls me over to her bed and stands on it. "Sit down."

I sit in front of her as I'm told. She wraps her legs around my shoulders. "Go to the stars." I brace her legs against me by holding onto her knees, and stand. We wobble slightly, and she giggles.

Once I have my footing, I walk us under that nightmare of a fake meteor shower. I stare at the wall until she says, "There." I bend my neck best I can with her on my shoulders and look up. Instead of "Bradley," the bottom stars read "Collins."

I dip and toss her off my shoulders, then catch her. She squeals a little, then laughs. Still holding her in my arms, I kiss her. Something hits my nose, and I flinch. Lacie pulls her head back, and we watch as several stars fall to the floor, along with a few specks of drywall.

"That's what happens when you try and restick DG stars after eight years." She shrugs, and we both laugh again.

I rock her in my arms. This is the best moment I've had since the cat catastrophe. We had a nice moment in the living room, but there were too many people milling around.

Lacie kicks her legs and hops down. "Let's go." She starts toward the door, bringing me back to reality. We have to go to another house with a lot of people. Oh, yay.

I follow her out of the room, and I don't protest this time when she flips off the light. Mrs. Sanderson rushes around the kitchen as we walk past.

"Is everything okay, Mama?"

"Yes." She answers Lacie without looking up from the stove. "I'm just triple checking to make sure all these stove eyes are off."

A horn honks outside. Mrs. Sanderson raises her head and huffs. "Hold your horses, Joey." She snatches her purse from counter and hurries out the front door.

"Why don't we take the Land Rover?" I suggest.

"Are you sure? You can't even open your door."

"So? I have to drive it home after tomorrow."

Lacie shrugs. "Okay."

I smile to myself. Now I have a way of leaving early if I want. Sometime at this next home, I need to get her dad off to the side and talk about the proposal. Then, if I can convince Lacie to leave with me, I can come back here and propose by the Christmas tree. There. Not ideal, but still a good plan.

Lacie waits as I climb in through the passenger door. After she gets in, I buckle my seat belt and turn to her. "Where to?"

"G-Maw's."

"Really? She just had like thirty people there last night. Isn't that a lot of hosting for someone her age?"

"Not G-Maw. She loves it."

"All right. At least I know how to get there." I smirk, then focus on backing up.

In a few minutes, we're at G-Maw's, walking up the AstroTurf ramp. Her house is pretty good-sized, but boxy. You can tell it was built way before open concept was a concept. It amazed me how all those people managed to squeeze in the den for Dirty Santa.

When Lacie opens the door, Woody greets us. He's holding Taco and Belle. Both are wearing tiny Santa hats, and I'm not sure how he got them to stay on their heads.

Woody is wearing a bright red-and-green Christmas sweater with dancing reindeer and a light-up collar.

"Hey, guys."

"Woody." I extend my hand. He shuffles the dogs enough to shake it. "Is this an ugly sweater party?"

"A what?" He cocks his head.

Oh shoot. I've just insulted his sweater, and he doesn't even realize it. "Oh, nothing. Nice dog hats." I point to Taco and Belle, then smile. He smiles back and nods.

Lacie smiles at Woody, too, then pulls me past him before I say anything else insulting. Once we're inside, the scent of buttered biscuits fills my nostrils. I halfway regret eating so many deer poppers. We eat at so many tapas places in Atlanta that I'd assumed Lacie's house was our only meal tonight.

"Well, Lacie and Collins." G-Maw steps between us and wraps us in a hug. She fits under my armpit, and I'm not even *that* tall. "Come, fix a plate. I made chicken and dumplings."

We go into the kitchen, where I expect to find an assortment of food like at Lacie's house. Nope. There are about ten pots of chicken and dumplings, along with six pans of biscuits. I raise my eyebrows. "Everyone brought the same thing?"

G-Maw swats at the air and laughs. "Of course not. I did all this."

"You? You made chicken and dumplings for forty people?"

She laughs. "Why, yeah. Mine are the best. I can't deprive anyone of not getting mine." She leans closer to us and whispers to Lacie, "But your sweet Mama offered to buy all the tea so I wouldn't have to make that."

I look at Lacie, and the corner of her mouth is raised. I can tell she's fighting off a laugh.

G-Maw pats Lacie on the arm and scurries off to greet more people. We fall in line and fix our bowls of dumplings. I spot Misty at the kitchen table, along with Earl, when we pour our tea.

I plan to sit by Earl, then change my mind when I overhear his and Misty's conversation.

"I told you to get a job. Alimony ain't gonna last you forever."

"I have a job."

"Impersonating Dolly Parton doesn't count."

"Tell that to all the people at Rudy Porter's retirement party last month."

I widen my eyes at Lacie. Her shoulders shake as she presses her lips to keep from laughing. We grab a few biscuits and speed walk toward the other end of the house.

We settle at a card table set up in the living room. This seems safer, as the only people in here are Jonah and Liam in the two recliners. They're watching some kind of wilderness show on TV. Earl's daughter and boyfriend come in a minute later and sit on the couch.

Lacie smiles at me from across the tiny table. "Only one more dinner stop, I promise."

"Okay." I take a bite of my dumplings and admire her cuteness. My eyes gravitate above her head to the rows of frames on the wall. A small, dark-haired girl stares back at me. "Is that you?"

She turns around and checks the photo, then laughs. She's wearing a white dress, with flowers in her hair. "Yep. That was Aunt Misty's fourth wedding. Or maybe her fifth. Anyway, whenever she married Jeffrey."

I chuckle as I imagine Misty and Jeffrey saying their vows. "You were cute."

"Thanks."

We eat our meal while I ask questions about other photos

and Lacie fills me in on all the details. Everything is going great until a bowl of dumplings shows up to my left. I recognize the long-sleeved tan shirt. I follow that sleeve up to a badge, then to Bradley's face.

"Evening, Collins and Lacie." He tips his hat in his weird Wild West way.

"Bradley." I nod, then look back at the photos and continue eating.

Bradley pulls out the chair between Lacie and me. He sits down and sighs. "Some day, huh?" When neither of us answers him, he continues talking. "You're looking much better, Collins. Or, not really better, but more like yourself." Bradley laughs.

Lacie bites off a chunk of her biscuit and rolls her eyes. Bradley stops laughing when nobody joins him. When he starts to speak again, I stand. I need a Bradley break before I break Bradley.

Lacie

I WATCH Collins stand and walk away. At first, I assume he's going to get another biscuit, but he heads for the front door. When the screen door creaks shut behind him, Bradley turns toward it and stares a moment, then looks at me. "Was it something I said?"

I shake my head at him. It probably was something he said, but I don't want to give Bradley the satisfaction of knowing that. I take the paper napkin from my lap and toss it on the table, then I pull on my coat and rush outside.

I find Collins at the edge of the AstroTurf, sitting in a

lawn chair. When I rest my hand on his shoulder, he swivels, almost tipping the chair over.

I kneel down beside him and ask the question that's made me a broken record these past few days. "Are you okay?"

He nods and exhales a frosty breath. "Yeah. I'm still a little dazed from that allergy episode and all the medication. I just needed some fresh air."

I lift the corner of my lips and rub his shoulder. "It can get a little stuffy at G-Maw's with so many people."

"Yeah." He lets out another breath and stares off into the night.

With the sky now covered in clouds—snow clouds, might I add—the only light in front of us is Woody's trailer. The door opens behind us, and I lift my head to see who it is. Carly has her head poked out and her body still inside. "G-Maw wanted me to find you guys and tell you we're about to play the Saran Wrap game."

"Okay, thanks." I grin at her, then drop my face back toward Collins.

"You go on and play."

I try to read his eyes, but it's too dark. Is he really not feeling well, or is he trying to get me to leave? I can't help but think this is less about Benadryl and more about Bradley. "Are you sure you don't want me to stay out here with you?"

He shakes his head. "I'll be in shortly."

I stand and fold my arms, lingering another moment, hoping he'll change his mind, then tiptoe inside. The living room is vacant except for Piper chasing around Taco and Belle in her diaper. I start to pick her up, but Woody comes in and gets her.

I give him an approving glance and head toward the den. I would say that Misty's lucky to have him in her life, except he's not really in her life. However, I get the feeling he really wants to be. Sure, he's bald and goofy, but if I were in her shoes, I'd jump at the chance to have Woody. At least he's a good man with a good job. That's way more than I can say for Jeffrey or any of her other exes.

The space covered with gifts last night is now bare, except for one huge ball of Saran Wrap. Everything from dollar bills, gift cards, and packs of gum stare back at us from inside the wrapping. There will be tons of Dollar General gems hidden inside as well, such as earbuds and dish towels. Pretty much anything small enough for G-Maw to fold inside a single layer.

"I can't believe we play this every year." G-Paw sits in the corner, shaking his head. "When I was a kid, only rich families had Saran Wrap. It's a shame how wasteful we are."

G-Maw pats his knee. "It's much cheaper now, Ed. And the kids love this game."

G-Paw folds his arms tighter across his belly. "Well, I ain't playin'."

"Suit yourself." G-Maw gives his knee one more pat and stands. "Okay, everyone, ready to play?" People of all ages cheer. "We start at one end of the room. Everyone unwraps one layer, then passes the ball. If a prize falls out on your turn, you can keep it."

She shuffles a few feet toward Carly, who is sitting on the floor near the ball. "Help me out dear." Carly crawls to the ball and tosses it in the air. It lands and rolls closest to Liam. He lets out a mock evil laugh and unwraps the first layer.

I watch a few minutes, then peek through the window. I can't get a good view of the front porch from here. I wonder if Collins is still outside. Someone taps me on the shoulder. I turn, hoping to see him. Instead, it's Krystal letting me know it's my turn. I pull back the plastic wrap, and a set of red press-on fingernails falls out. I hold it up for everyone to see, which is customary in this game. Some people ohhh and ahhh as if I've unwrapped the keys to a new Mercedes.

I go back to my spot near the window, settle back in my chair, and glance around the room. Collins is standing in the doorway. I motion for him to come in. He walks behind the crowd and stands behind me. "Feel better?"

"Yeah." He smiles down at me.

I smile back, then relax my shoulders. My nerves jolt when I hear the distinctive noise of Bradley's truck cranking up. I'm glad he's gone, but I wonder if he and Collins had an exchange before Collins came back inside.

I pick at my fingernail polish and try not to think about it. Good thing I just got fake nails. Applause breaks out around me, bringing my attention back to the game. Daddy unravels the last bit of the wrapping. A toy truck falls out, and everyone laughs. He tosses it to a young boy sitting across the room. One of the homeschool kids from down the road.

Collins puts his hands on my shoulders, and I rest one my hands on his. I close my eyes for a second and pray that everything is okay with him. On the bright side of things, I can't imagine anything else possibly going wrong.

CHAPTER FIFTEEN

Collins

I'll admit it. The only reason I went back into G-Maw's house was because Bradley left. If that makes me sound like an adolescent girl rather than a grown man, then please, take my man card. I've had about enough of that guy.

As soon as he walked out the front door, I narrowed my eyes and flared my nostrils. Like a bull seeing red, I was ready to fight. He glanced my way for a split second, then went to his truck. If he'd said just one word, I'd have lit into him.

I was so sure of it that I stood and went inside before he could walk back past me. My Christmas wish was granted when I heard his redneck ride rev up in the yard. Not that it means he won't show up again. But it gives me a few moments without his looming presence.

Lacie offers to help G-Maw put away everything as people start leaving. We rake all the leftover dumplings into two massive pots. G-Maw opens the refrigerator and starts handing me things to hold while she makes space for the dumplings. We manage to get everything back inside, but I'm not sure how. If anyone wants dumplings, they'll have to move about five things to get to them.

"What about all this sweet tea?" Lacie cocks her head toward the leftover tea on the kitchen counter.

G-Maw taps her finger on her lips. "Take it to the cellar."

"Okay." Lacie starts gathering armfuls of tea, and I do the same. She waddles toward the back of the den, and I follow. G-Maw shuffles to get in front of us and open a door. She flips a switch, then moves for us to go downstairs.

We take our time descending the narrow stairway without rails. I can see now why G-Maw is scared of falling. They should AstroTurf this place instead of the porch.

We make it down to a cold concrete floor. There are three deep freezers and two refrigerators. "Wow."

"G-Maw's really into freezing meat and vegetables."

"I'll say. We're coming here during the apocalypse."

Lacie laughs. "Between this and G-Paw's gun safe, it's about the best place to be."

She squats and sets down her jugs of tea. I do the same. Mrs. Sanderson went a little overboard on buying tea. She must really hate her mom's.

Lacie opens one of the refrigerator doors and pushes a few jars of pickles to the side. Not the normal jars people keep at home, but the huge jars you see in the back of concession stands. "Can you hand me the teas?" she asks.

"Yep." I bend down and turn to get some. When I do, my hand touches a glass jar with a pig face inside, making me jump back and rub my hands together.

Lacie bursts out laughing. I stare at the jar and scratch the back of my head. "Is that the pig head jelly?"

Once Lacie calms down from laughing, she says, "Nope, that's a science project."

"What in the world?"

"It was Aunt Misty's biology project in college."

I lift my eyebrows. I'm more surprised that Aunt Misty went to college than I am that this pig was a science project.

"She was supposed to dissect the pig fetus. She refused to and failed the class. G-Paw got so mad at her that he brought the jar home. He told her it would stay right here in the cellar until she decided to dissect it. If she did, he'd give her a hundred dollars. That was his way of trying to motivate her to not quit things. Thirty years later and it's still here."

"Well, that explains a lot." I bend down for the tea, keeping an eye out for the pig. With all the surgeries I perform on a daily basis, I'm not scared of a dead or open body. But there's something extra freaky about a pickled pig in a basement.

Once the teas are put away, we head for the stairs and make our way back to ground level. G-Maw is wiping down tables, while G-Paw is picking up shreds of Saran Wrap. I swear I hear him cursing under his breath.

"Thank you, Lacie and Collins. We'll see you kids in a minute," G-Maw says.

"You're welcome." Lacie hugs her grandma, and we go out to my SUV.

We're the only people still here, except for Woody and Misty. She's buckling her baby into a car seat, while Woody lets the dogs pee. We wave to them, then get in the vehicle and drive away.

"Go past my house to the end of the road."

"Okay." I pass the Sandersons' house and drive maybe another two miles. At the end of the road is a huge brick house with immaculate landscaping, including a fountain out front. "Wow." It's like the southern version of the *Home Alone* house.

"Yeah, Uncle Earl likes to spend everything he makes."

"I can see that."

Lacie sighs. "He justifies it by saying the chances of his kids going to college are slim to none."

I widen my eyes. There's nothing nice I can say to that. I turn off the engine and wait for Lacie to get out, then I crawl through and shut the door.

Christmas music plays, from where I'm not sure. After a few seconds, I notice the walkway lights are synchronized to the tune. I bet that cost a pretty penny.

Lacie stops at the fountain and runs her hand across the frozen water inside. "Looky here. It's already below freezing." She arches a brow and smirks.

I shake my head and keep walking. That girl and her weather. We climb the oversized steps up to the front porch. I open one of the double doors, which are about twelve feet tall. Gold ribbons and lights blur my vision as soon as we enter the foyer. I notice a coat rack on one side of the doors. "Here." I help Lacie out of her jacket, and take off mine, hanging them both on empty pegs.

I hear something to our right and peek my head in a room. It's a theater room with a big screen. Some kids are in there watching *The Santa Clause*. I contemplate slipping in the back and riding this last party out in there, but I follow Lacie on toward the kitchen like a good boyfriend.

The kitchen countertops are covered with decorative cookies. I'm sure Carla is behind those. Another table is filled with pies, and another with cakes. A lone pan sits near the sink. "What's that?"

Lacie turns in the direction I'm looking. "Oh! That's crack."

"Excuse me?"

"Cookie crack."

I rub my chin and wonder for a split second if this really has something illegal in it. "Why is it here by itself?"

Lacie laughs. "We bring it out one pan at a time, because everyone goes crazy over it. That's why we call it crack."

Lacie tiptoes over to the pan and cuts a piece. She brings it back and raises it to my mouth. I bite off a piece and begin to chew. This might be the best thing that's ever hit my mouth.

"Who makes it?"

"A woman from my parents' church."

I lick my fingers, not caring that I'm eating something called crack, or that this crack originated from a church lady. It. Is. Good.

We walk over to the punch bowl and get some cups of green slush. "This is Christmas punch. It's tastes like a limeade slush," Lacie says.

"Cool." I take a sip, then down the entire cup. Not that I'm a huge limeade fan, but that crack left my mouth dry. Lacie gets a Christmas tree cookie, and I ask her to get me more crack. She giggles and crosses the kitchen for another piece.

I stare up at the tall ceiling and fancy chandelier. Everything in the Sandersons' home is wooden and cozy. This house is all white and granite. It's a beautiful home, but not as welcoming.

"Your crack, sir," Lacie says as she returns.

"Thank you." I bite off a huge piece and let out a little moan.

Lacie laughs. "It is addictive."

We make our way toward the living area, where a lot of people are gathered. Lacie starts talking to Annette from the Angel Tree. I put my hands in my pockets and survey the room, not wanting to get in on their conversation. I spot Mr.

Sanderson alone in the corner eating a piece of pie. This is my chance. It's already nine o'clock. It's now or never.

I cross the room, fumbling with the ring box on my way. Halfway across the room, a few kids run in front of me. I stop to keep from knocking them down. After they move past, Mr. Sanderson is gone. I jerk my head, trying to find him. I see the back of his shirt near the hallway and head that way.

From a non-creepy distance—at least I hope—I follow him down a long hallway. He turns to go in a room on the left. I rush up to the door and open it.

To Bradley. Holding a gun.

Man, I can't catch a break. I glance around his head. The room behind him is covered wall to wall in guns and ammo. I stand corrected. This would be the place to go during the apocalypse.

"What are you doing here?" Bradley lifts his chin, which is the cocky human equivalent to a dog lifting its leg.

"What are *you* doing here?" I reply.

He smirks. "Checking out Earl's new gun. He wanted me to see it, since we were talking about the gun club banquet."

"Oh." Well, dang. He has a reason. So do I, but not one I care to share with Bradley.

"Now answer my question."

I cut my eyes past Bradley to try and see Mr. Sanderson. All I see is a long room lined with guns. For all I know, it leads to some secret tunnel. I move my eyes to meet Bradley's. He's irritated. All I can manage to say is, "Uh, do you know where the bathroom is?"

He lifts the hand holding the gun and points it beside my ear. "First door, across the hall."

I duck my head away from the gun and back up. After he shuts the door, I retreat to the bathroom. With no better plan, I decide to wait in here until I hear Mr. Sanderson's voice.

The bathroom is relatively small compared to the rest of the house. I shut the door and pass time sitting on top of the toilet seat, thumbing through a magazine called *Garden & Gun*. Pretty interesting stuff.

Halfway into reading about ducks, I hear voices, so I hop up and set the magazine on the counter. I open the door, expecting to see Mr. Sanderson. Instead, I see the back of Lacie's head and the top of Bradley's hat.

I ease back inside the bathroom and keep the door cracked. I'm so an adolescent girl right now. But I don't care. I can't make out what they're saying, so I watch through the slither of open space.

Bradley puts his arms around Lacie's shoulders. Okay, I've had enough. I fling open the door, ready to beat that stupid Rick Grimes hat off his fat head. Then I freeze. They're kissing.

I want to punch him, yell at her, throw the ring at their heads. Something. Anything. But I can't. That's not me. I don't cause scenes or pitch fits. Instead, I take a deep breath and race down the hallway, through the living room, out the front door, and past the dancing lights.

I only stop when I run into the old cowboy who's always fixing to-go plates. He drops his box, and crack hits the cobblestone walkway. He moans. I mutter "sorry" and keep running until I get to my Land Rover. Then I crawl in through the passenger door.

I slam the door best I can and slide across to the driver's seat. Then I head to Lacie's house to gather my things and go home.

Lacie

MY MOUTH FEELS like I'm swallowing a dead fish. I put my hands on Bradley's chest and shove him toward the wall. Then I reach out and slap his jaw. He stares at me like I'm crazy.

"What were you doing?"

"Kissing you. Or trying to." He rubs his jawline and frowns.

"Why?" I jerk my head and scoff.

"Because, I wanted to."

I roll my eyes. "Had it ever occurred to you that I *didn't* want you to kiss me?"

Bradley touches his lips. The faint creases in the corners of his eyes deepen. I genuinely think my opinion on the matter never crossed his mind.

"I'm with Collins. I love Collins. You've known that the whole time we've been here. The only reason I talked to you just now was to ask if you'd seen him. What would ever possess you to think I'd want to kiss *you*?"

"Lacie, can you honestly say you don't have feelings for me?"

I laugh—a hysterical, creepy laugh. I've never heard that kind of sound come out of my body, but I'm glad it did, because Bradley backs up a step and tilts his head away from me. But I'm not letting that jerk off this easy. I get in his face and poke my finger in his chest.

"I have feelings for you, all right. I feel sorry for you. All these years, and you go around sucking up to everyone in Wisteria like you're still the quarterback. You even still wear that stupid championship ring."

Bradley spreads his fingers and glances down at his foot-ball ring from high school.

"When are you finally going to grow up, Bradley? Quit thinking everything is the same as it was in high school. It's not. We're adults. And I don't want some cocky kid. I want a kind, mature man." I drop my finger from his chest and clinch my jaw. Then I turn on my heels and march into the living area.

In a house this big with so many people, my best bet is to ask around. I walk around, twisting my head toward every group of people, and notice my parents standing on the heated patio outside the kitchen. I open the glass door and go to them. They're talking to Brother Billy and a few more people from church.

"Sorry to interrupt, but has anyone seen Collins?"

Mama bites her bottom lip and scans the yard before settling her eyes back on me. "No, baby. Is something wrong?"

I shake my head. "Thanks anyway." I don't want to worry Mama, especially not on Christmas Eve. I jog toward the front of the house. There's an empty space where his SUV was parked earlier. I rush back inside and find Liam walking into the theater room. "Liam, I need your help." My words come out breathless.

He puts his hands on my arms. "Whoa, what's wrong?" I must sound desperate if Liam is concerned.

"I can't find Collins, and his vehicle is gone."

"Okay, maybe he went back to our place."

I nod. "Yeah, do you mind driving me there?"

"Uh, sure. Just one minute." Liam sticks his head inside the theater room. "Carly, tell your friend I'll text her later."

I sigh and grab his wrist. "Come on, please. You can flirt with underage girls later."

"She's almost eighteen."

I roll my eyes and rush him out the door. We climb in his truck and peel out of the yard toward our house. When we get there, I don't see the Land Rover. I hop out of the truck, not even bothering to shut the door.

Liam gets out and shuts both our doors. "Maybe he parked around back."

That's highly doubtful since he hasn't ever, and we moved him out of the basement. Nonetheless, Liam and I make our way to the backyard. The motion lights come on at side of the house. Liam starts calling Collins's name.

I snap my head back at him and grit my teeth.

"What?"

"He's not a dog."

"So? He has a name."

I shake my head and continue walking. We make the entire loop around the house. No sign of the Land Rover. No sign of Collins.

When we get back to the front, I go inside. Liam follows me. We check my room first. I hold my breath when I see his things missing from the corner of the room.

"What happened?" Liam whispers behind me.

I swallow, trying to fight back tears. It doesn't work. I sniffle to catch my breath, then cry out, "He's gone."

Liam puts his hand on my shoulder. I turn and bury my head against his skinny chest. He slowly lifts his arms until he's hugging me, and I stand there crying until I can manage to catch my breath.

I pull back and Liam blinks at me. He's never seen me like this before. "Hey, I'll go look for him."

I run the back of my hand across my face to wipe it dry. "No use. I just need to lie down a while."

Liam nods and backs out of my room. I turn off the lights, lie back on my bed, and close my eyes. I have no idea where Collins is or why, but he left and took everything with him. That means he isn't coming back. Even worse, he didn't say goodbye. That means he doesn't want to see me.

I open my eyes, sending a fresh stream of tears down my cheeks. On the ceiling glows "Lacie N Co ns." I laugh deliriously from anger, hurt, and exhaustion. Then I roll over and bury my head in my pillow.

Stupid Wisteria and my redneck family have struck again.

CHAPTER SIXTEEN

Collins

I drive out of Wisteria, toward Apple Cart. My low-fuel light starts glowing. Just great. I don't want to chance getting stuck in rural Alabama, so I turn back. I'm closer to the gas station in Wisteria than anywhere else. While my GPS is still picking up a signal, I search the quickest route to the Quick Stop, which points to a side road.

All it takes for me to decide I want to chance this unknown route is a few flurries hitting my windshield. The last thing I need is to sleep in my car on Christmas Eve because the roads froze over. Lacie must be over the moon right now. She's probably sitting on the back porch of her uncle's mansion, watching it snow with Bradley.

Ugh. I want to vomit.

My nerves twitch when I think about the ring in my pocket. If it weren't my grandmother's, I'd sell it to Pop's pawn shop.

It's snowing enough now to where I need my windshield wipers. I continue on the narrow path, slowing down when one of my wipers sticks. Must be a side effect of the wreck. I come to an older bridge and with trees swaying on either side. I ease across it for fear I might slide off if I drive normal speed. I've almost made it across, when I hear a loud snap, and a huge cedar falls across the hood of my vehicle.

My head jerks back as the airbag pops out. I rub my forehead where it grazed against me. Thanks to the powdery smell and the unexpected impact, I really do have to vomit now. I struggle to unbuckle my seat belt, then make it to the passenger side. I open the door and spill my guts. Unfortunately, not all of it lands outside of my car.

Then I climb out over the mess and slam the door. The car lights highlight the falling snow. The flakes are falling faster by the minute. I circle to the front of my car and survey the damage.

I stand and take a few steps back. The entire front is busted, one tire is flat, and the bumper lies in the road. I slap a hand on my forehead and suck in a long, icy breath. With no other options, I go back inside and grab my phone. I search for an Uber nearby, but nothing pops up. I google for a tow truck. Nothing.

I pull up my GPS. The gas station is over a mile. I could walk it and have the honor of telling my future grandkids that I once walked a mile in the snow. But that seems a little overkill for a cliché story. According to my phone, there's a hotel and restaurant only a third of a mile away. It's just outside of Wisteria. If I walk there, I can ask about a tow truck or an Uber. Worst case scenario, I can get some sleep someplace besides the puke-mobile.

Just in case, I pull my suitcase from the back and hook my external battery to my phone. Then I turn off my vehicle and zip up my coat. I use my phone's flashlight to lead me to the location of the Quality Inn.

The snow peppers my face. Whatever heat was left on my skin from the cat allergy is now frozen. I blink the wet flakes from my eyelids and focus on the road ahead. The hairs on my neck stand taller with every sound that comes from the woods. I could use one of Earl's guns about now. Growing up in suburban Atlanta, I didn't exactly take nature walks. Especially in pitch dark when it was snowing.

After a few more yards, I see a light up ahead. And good thing, because my phone service goes to nothing. It may as well be the Christmas star, because that light is all I need to power walk the last bit of this journey. I smile at the prospect of escaping the snow as the road comes to an end.

I step out into a vast parking lot with only a few cars and turn to face one long building that's clearly three places in one. Kind of like a strip mall, but without the usual vape place and Subway. No chain businesses on these three signs. The first sign reads, "Quality Inn," with the word "Quality" blinking in and out. The next area has a light-up sign that reads, "The Hole." The last part of the building has a wooden sign that reads, "Enchilada." I've heard the Sandersons mention Enchilada a few times, so maybe it's not so sketchy. I stare a few minutes, contemplating which door to enter, then the "Quality" fizzles out completely, so that I'm looking at "Inn The Hole Enchilada."

Well, that pretty much sums up my time in Wisteria. I drop my head and pull my suitcase toward the inn. There's a paper sign taped to the door. "Use Next Door." I roll my suitcase over to The Hole and open the door. It's a liquor store with low lighting. Now I really need one of Earl's guns.

I shake the snow from my head and glance behind the counter for someone. There's nothing but cases of alcohol. I start out the door, but a guy's voice calls behind me, "Come through this way."

I turn around to see an open glass door at the back of the liquor room. This is shaping up like a horror movie, but what choice do I have? I swallow and step through the doorway. I'm now standing beside the register in a Mexican restaurant, which has to be Enchilada.

A few other people are there, sitting on a bench in the corner. A young woman walks out with several plastic bags. "Order for Rudy." She looks at a paper-thin guy with a face tattoo, who's holding a duffle bag.

He shakes his head. "I'm here for a room."

"Oh, over there." She motions toward the register with her head. He goes up to the register, and she calls louder, "Order for Rudy."

An old man raises his hand and takes the bag.

"Merry Christmas," the woman says.

He nods, then heads out into the snow. Not sure what else to do, I get in line behind the skinny guy needing a room. I suddenly have extra sympathy for Mary and Joseph.

The guy behind the counter—the one who called me in —gives Face Tattoo a key. He enters the dining area, and I step up to the register. "Hi, I broke down not far from here. Do you know where I can find a tow truck?"

The guy runs a hand through his hair and puffs up his cheeks. "On Christmas Eve?"

"Yeah." It's not like I have much choice in the matter.

"Uh, I could call Kyle, but he's probably asleep."

"Does anyone nearby drive for Uber?"

"Uh." He scratches his head. "I think Earl Ed is the only Uber driver around here."

Of course he is. I try and stay calm.

He frowns and taps his pen on the counter. "Look, you

seem like a nice guy. Why don't you get some food, and I'll try and find someone to help you."

"Thanks." I press my lips into a sad smile, then roll my suitcase up to the bar.

A middle-aged man with a handlebar mustache and Popeye muscles stands behind the bar wiping out glasses. The boy from the front comes up to him and says, "Hey, give this guy a discount. He's having a rough time."

Popeye nods. He puts down the glass he's cleaning and leans across the counter. "You want the special."

"What's the special?"

"Trust me." He winks. "You want it."

"Okay, but what is it?"

He starts spinning a margarita glass between his fingers. He's very agile for someone with such large hands. Then he fixes a margarita and slides it my way. "One margarita, one enchilada dinner, and one night's stay." He winks again. "That's the special."

Against my better judgment, I nod and take a sip of the drink. Here I am at Inn The Hole Enchilada to escape the snow, drinking a girly drink after wrecking yet again and puking in my SUV.

I can now say I've officially hit rock bottom.

Lacie

I LIE ON MY BED, staring at the ceiling, then jump up and turn on the lights. I can't take any more of those cheesy stars glowing down at me.

I return to my bed, stare at my phone, and spend the

next ten minutes in a cycle of reaching for it to call Collins and talking myself out of it. He doesn't want to hear from me. He left me. No note, no explanation, no goodbye. Just up and left.

Maybe instead of blaming my hometown, or my family, I should blame him. If he isn't man enough to deal with the kind of crap that comes with everyday life, then I don't need him.

I grab my phone again, but not to call Collins. I want to check the time. It's already eleven-thirty. Aside from last year when I was working in Atlanta, I haven't missed a Christmas Eve candlelight service ever. My life is a mess, but I'm not one to break tradition. Besides, what better place to feel sorry for myself than church?

I stand and put my phone back in my pocket. Then I grab my coat from where I flung it by my bed and leave my room. Mama is sitting on the couch, watching the rest of *The Christmas Shoes*.

"Mama, again?"

She sniffs and blots her eyes. "I just wanted to finish it before church."

I raise my eyes to the ceiling and laugh.

She peers over the back of the couch. "Where's Collins, asleep?"

I shake my head. "He left."

Mama pauses her movie and turns all the way around. "He what?"

"He left."

"Well, you should've told me he was leaving. I would've told him bye."

I lift my hand to stop her. "Mama."

"You didn't know he was leaving, did you?"

I lower my head. Before I lift it, Mama is around the couch, hugging me. "Oh, baby. I'm so sorry."

I hug her back and rest my head on her shoulder. A few more tears fall from my eyes as I blink them against her soft sweater. Mama strokes my hair and hugs me tighter. After a few minutes, I regain a little composure and pull back.

Mama rests her hands on my shoulders and focuses on my eyes. "Now, I will stay here with you if you want. Or you can stay by yourself. You—"

"It's okay, Mama." I put my hands on hers. "Really, I think church would make me feel better."

She presses her lips together and grips my hands. Then she releases me and nods. "You can ride with us."

I lift my mouth into a tired grin.

"Come on, the boys are already in the garage." We walk out to Daddy and Liam taking inventory of all the hog-killing equipment for tomorrow morning. "It's time to go to church," Mama says.

Daddy takes the knife from Liam and sets it beside the meat grinders. Then we all get in his truck. On the way to church, nobody mentions Collins. I've talked about him with both Liam and Mama already. Either Daddy knows and he's being polite about it, or he's clueless. Probably the latter, knowing Daddy.

We're almost in town when flurries pepper the wind-shield. Daddy turns on the wipers. Liam stares out his window and asks, "Is that snow?"

I smile. "Yep, just like I said."

We get to the church, and I watch as the flurries hit the pavement and melt. According to the weather patterns, the ground should be frozen by now. A sickness swirls in my stomach. It's snowing like I said it would. But I expected this to be the Alabama snow of the century, not some powdered sugar flakes here and there.

I pull my coat closer around my neck and follow my family into the church. Brother Billy greets us at the door and hands us all a candle. I take one last look outside before we move ahead to find seats. First Bradley makes a move on me, then Collins runs away, and now my much-anticipated snowstorm isn't much of a storm . . . or a snow. For the first time in my life, Christmas Eve isn't my favorite day.

CHAPTER SEVENTEEN

Collins

I push my margarita to the side and drop my head in my hands. It tastes horrible, and not just because I don't drink anymore. Or because I've never liked margaritas. It's because everything is horrible right now.

I should've stayed home and visited my parents. By now, we'd be on our second showing of *A Christmas Story*, bellies full of steak and potatoes. Instead, I'm at a bar in the middle of nowhere, sipping a nasty cocktail.

Merry Christmas Eve to me.

Just when I'm thinking my life can't get any worse, someone sits on the stool beside me. I slant my eyes and almost fall off my own stool when I see a tan cowboy hat and a sheriff's badge. I drag the nasty margarita in front of my face. I'll sacrifice taste for my sanity.

"Hot plate!" The guy from the register brings out an enchilada the size of Popeye's forearm, along with rice, beans, chips, and salsa. He sets it in front of me. "Need anything else?"

"A fork." Which should be obvious. "And maybe some water?" I'm not falling off the wagon over Bradley. He nods and heads back toward the front.

"I see you got the special."

I ignore Bradley and focus on the neon bar signs and paper cactus hanging over the bar. My fork and water arrive, and I thank the guy. Then I drain half the glass of water in one gulp, slam the cup on the bar, and sigh.

"So, I get a call saying there's a cedar tree and a fancy SUV blocking Broken Bridge. Then I get a call from Johnny up front, saying there's a guy here who needs some help. I put two and two together, and well, I'm here for whatever you need."

I stab my fork in the enchilada and spin on my stool to face him. "What I need is for you to stay out of my business. Ever since we met, you've been trying to belittle me or embarrass me. Then you go and kiss my girlfriend on Christmas Eve when I'm in the bathroom."

Popeye stops stacking glasses and looks down at Bradley. "Man, that's not cool."

"It's not how he makes it sound, Pete."

Popeye—uh, Pete—folds his arms and stares at us. "Then tell me your side."

I spin back toward the bar and pick at my enchilada, refusing to look at Bradley. That way, I can at least say he lied behind my back instead of to my face.

"He's dating Lacie."

"Your Lacie?"

Uh, really, Pete?

"Yeah." Bradley grabs a handful of my chips. That of all things pushes me over the edge.

"Seriously? You kiss my girlfriend, and then you steal my chips? Do you want my germs that bad?"

Bradley raises his hands. "Let me finish."

I snarl and pull my food out of his reach.

"Kissing Lacie was a mistake. She slapped me."

I laugh around a mouthful of rice.

"Did she give you any signals that she wanted you to kiss her?" Pete poses a great question. I take it this isn't his first rodeo.

Bradley glances at the ceiling, then shakes his head. He looks back at Pete, then me. "No."

"Then why would you kiss a girl who didn't show interest in you and who has a boyfriend?" Pete nods at me, then frowns at Bradley.

Bradley shrinks his shoulders and props his elbows on the bar. "I don't know. History, I guess? I haven't dated anyone seriously since her, and I guess I never got over her breaking up with me."

Pete unfolds his arms and props his hands on the bar. "Is that because you still love her or because it hurt your ego to get dumped?"

Wow. Pete's a regular redneck Dr. Phil. He's over here unpacking Bradley's pain, while I snack on chips and enjoy the show.

Bradley taps his fingers on the bar as if this is the first time he's considered that. After a long minute of Pete and I waiting for an answer, he sighs. "Come to think of it, I guess you're right, Pete. My whole life, I've been the best at everything, the star. I've won at everything. Except for my relationship with Lacie. I would've probably married her . . . eventually. But not so much out of love as because I thought she made my life better. She was hot and smart. I wanted a girl of that status."

I reach for my water before I choke on Bradley's words.

Never in a million years would I guess a guy this cocky could be so vulnerable. Pete deserves a medal for his work.

I swallow my drink and turn to Bradley. "So you're not still in love with Lacie?"

Bradley shrugs. "I only think about her when I see her."

I flare my nostrils and clench my jaw. "You mean to tell me that you kissed her just because you saw her again? Because you think she's hot?"

"Pretty much."

I ball up a fist to hit Bradley. Instead, I shove my hand in my pocket and bring out the ring box. I slam it on the bar between us. Bradley and Pete stare at the box, then slowly raise their eyes to me.

"I was planning on proposing tonight." I flip the box open. "With my grandmother's ring."

"Dude, I didn't know."

I snatch up the box, closing the lid as I put it back in my pocket. "It doesn't matter that you didn't know. And it doesn't matter whether I was going to propose or not. You kissed my girlfriend, whom you dated for a very long time. That's just wrong."

I pull a ten out of my wallet and slap it on the bar. "Thanks, Pete."

Pete nods, pity now in his squinty eyes.

I stand and drain the last of my water. Then I rush out of the bar, pulling my suitcase behind me. Forget the Uber. Forget the tow truck. I'd rather walk home, or rot in Wisteria, than depend on Bradley for help.

When I exit the restaurant, the cold hits me like a brick wall. The snowflakes are thicker than before, and there's a dusting on the sidewalk. I hunch my shoulders as I brave the cold a few more feet to Room 6, where it looks like I'll be spending Christmas. Lucky me.

Lacie

"SILENT NIGHT" fills the sanctuary of Wisteria Worship Center as we join together to sing the traditional closing song for the candlelight service. Every year, our church gathers to sing and pray in Christmas morning.

I stare ahead at the stained-glass image of Jesus glistening in the candlelight. This song, this night, usually brings me such peace. But tonight my mind is a mud pit of everything that's gone wrong. Why would Collins leave me like that? If he didn't like my family, he could've at least had the decency to tell me.

The song ends, and Brother Billy climbs the steps to the pulpit. The bald spot on the back of his head shines when the candlelight hits it. He faces the congregation and instructs everyone to take a seat.

I lower myself onto the pew. The people in front of us have two small kids standing on the pew. The man grabs the kids' candles. The little boy pouts and squats to jump, but his mom grabs hold of his shirt and tugs him down into his seat. Then she pulls the little girl into her lap.

My cheeks warm as I observe them. I'd been sure I'd marry Collins in the near future, and we'd eventually have children of our own. Now I'm not so sure. I put my free hand in my coat pocket and feel my phone. I want so badly to text him, but I don't want to beg him back.

If he calls me first, or better yet, comes back . . .

I need a sign that he's all in. If I contact him first, he might pity me. I've got to stand my ground. This wasn't some silly fight. He packed up and left without any notice. On

Christmas Eve. When he'd come to spend Christmas with me.

I sigh and drop my shoulders. People all around me bow their heads. I do the same and actually focus on what Brother Billy is saying. He prays a rather lengthy prayer, ending with how God is in control. That gives me a shred of hope, despite my whole world turning upside down in a day.

Brother Billy says "amen," and we all repeat it. He asks that we exit the church in a moment of silence.

One by one, we leave the sanctuary. The only sound is the subtle shuffle of coats brushing by and shoes crossing the carpeted floor. The only sight is the candles lighting our way. An unexpected calm washes over me. A sense that everything will be okay, no matter what. I pray that it will.

We blow out our candles and toss them in the box in foyer like we do each year. It's now Christmas morning. I swallow back my emotions and follow my family onto the porch. It's still flurrying outside, which makes me smile a little.

"Look!" One of the kids from the pew in front of us points to the manger scene. There's a thin layer of snow on Mary and Joseph. "Snow!" He rushes over and wipes at Mary's head with his hand. His mom follows and makes sure he doesn't damage the display.

I smile as his sister toddles over to join him. There's a good chance these kids have never seen snow before. It's not the snow I'd hoped it would be for them, or me. But it's real snow.

As more and more people step out into the church parking lot, they point to the snow. Some older people complain, but most laugh and embrace the flakes falling on their heads. Brother Billy comes out on the porch and laughs as well. He lifts his arms. "What a glorious blessing the Lord has given us. A white Christmas. Let's sing together."

He starts an off-key rendition of "White Christmas." Luckily, the guitar player is still here. He unzips his case and starts playing. Then a few choir members take over, drowning out Brother Billy. The rest of us join in as we watch the snow.

Everyone is caught up in the moment. Except for maybe Liam, who blurts out in the middle of the chorus, "Hey, does anyone know where I can get a four-inch lift kit for my truck?" We all ignore him.

Old couples have gone from complaining to slow dancing beneath the street lights. G-Maw has abandoned her cane to clap along. Little kids are twirling around with their tongues out. And . . . oh my.

Aunt Misty and Woody are making out on the hood of his car. Oh well, good for them. It's Christmas.

And it's high time I went to sleep to try and forget what a dumpster fire my life is right now.

CHAPTER EIGHTEEN

Collins

I jiggle the rusty key in the lock until the door opens to Room 6. When it does, it almost falls off the hinges. I sniff the air. A combination of cigarettes and mold meets my nose. Just lovely.

I shut the door behind me and turn the lock. At least I know it works. Then I park my suitcase by the bed and head for the bathroom. Above the toilet, at eye level, is a stuffed squirrel holding an acorn. I jump. Not what I expected to see.

There's not a single other decoration in the entire room, but they plant a squirrel to scare someone into peeing on the seat.

I shake my head and go about my business, then go to the main room for my toiletries bag. A shower should help. I return to the bathroom and pull the shower curtain. Well, I found the mold.

I make a quick decision to shower in my socks. There's no way I'm stepping my bare feet in that shower. And I didn't exactly pack sandals since it's late December.

Wouldn't you know it, but there's no hot water. I lather up with soap as quickly as I can and shampoo my hair in record time. Then I huddle under the freezing water, wearing nothing but socks and a face full of disgust.

I was wrong earlier. *This* is rock bottom.

As soon as I see suds-less water hit the tub, I cut the faucet and hop out. My wet socks slip on the linoleum floor. I grab hold of the towel rack hanging above the toilet. I still fall, taking the towel rack and the squirrel down with me.

The squirrel and I are eye-to-eye again. I grab it and chunk it in the tub, and pull the towel from the rack. I dry off best I can, then somehow manage to steady the towel rack back in the drywall. That should stay at least until the next guest tries to get a towel.

I frown at the soggy squirrel lying in the bottom of the draining tub. Serves it right, scaring me twice.

I brush my teeth, then I lay my towel across the sink, which is thankfully mold free. I hold onto the doorframe, G-Maw style, to make it across to the carpeted floor of my bedroom. A roach runs in front of me, so I change from wet socks to dry socks before putting on any more clothes.

I barely have my pajamas on when someone knocks on the door. I roll my eyes. Probably a drunk who's got the wrong room. I hear one more knock and sit on the edge of the bed. If I'm quiet, they'll eventually go away.

"Collins, I know you're in there."

Okay, I didn't expect them to know my name. I tiptoe to the widow and peek through the blinds, which are stiff and beige and smell like an ashtray. I expected as much, but I didn't expect to find Bradley staring at me.

I jerk my head back and let go of the blinds. They clink

against the window as they fall back into place. The door handle starts jiggling. I stand by and smile as Bradley attempts to break in. My smile fades when he opens the door a few seconds later.

I grab the nearby floor lamp and hold it over my head to whack him. The lamp cord jerks from the wall socket. When it does, the other lamp and the florescent light in the bathroom start blinking. Then a loud buzz hums overhead and all the lights go out. Just great.

Bradley switches on the light on his phone. "Don't think so highly of yourself. It's probably the storm and not you pulling that cord."

That's it. I bring the lamp down full force toward Bradley's head. He dodges, and it hits across the threshold, breaking the bulb onto the sidewalk.

A few flecks of glass land on Bradley's boot. He shakes his foot, and they blend into the snow. "Yeah, you're not getting your security deposit back."

I let go of the lamp and seethe with anger. "Will you please just leave me alone? You've ruined my relationship, knocked me off a tractor, made a fool of me at the ornament shooting. Need I say more?"

"Now hold on, big dog. Liam gave you the gun. And you fell off that tractor."

I ball up my fist and swing at him. He dodges again, and I slide on the icy sidewalk and fall flat on my butt. My butt had just gotten better from Bully's bite, but now it's throbbing again.

Bradley offers me a hand. I slap it away and stumble to standing, gritting my teeth when I step on shards of broken glass with my sock feet. Bradley shakes his head. He kicks the lampstand out of the way and shoves me back inside the room.

He points to the bed. "Sit." He uses the same tone as

when he first pulled me over. I can see a seriousness sweep across his face. Maybe it's the effects of the phone flashlight. Regardless, he has my attention. Besides, I refuse to fight in the dark against anyone that good at dodging punches.

"I'm an idiot. But so are you," he says.

"I—"

"Listen, or I'll arrest you."

"For what?"

"For being an idiot."

I lock my jaw and flare my nostrils. I'll sit here and pretend to listen if that's what it takes for him to leave.

"Pete proved to me what an idiot I've been. I never loved Lacie like I should've, and I'm not right for her. She's bigger than this place, and I always knew it. I was just hanging onto her long as I could because she was familiar." He wavers his head. "And hot. But you can't entirely blame me for that, since we were young."

I nod. I'm actually listening now, as Bradley pointing out his own faults proves to be really therapeutic.

"I was an idiot for making a move on her. She let me know it, Pete let me know it, and you let me know it. If I could go back to that first day I pulled you over and reset how I've acted, I would, but I can't. But you can reset things —with Lacie. And you're an idiot if you don't."

I fall back on the bed and cup my hands over my face. "I left without telling anyone. I just grabbed my things and headed out of town like a coward. She'll never take me back."

Bradley huffs. "Dude, give her some credit. She's more understanding than that. She stayed with me through a lot, which I didn't deserve. I think she can forgive your one incident."

I drop my hands from my face. "You think?"

"Yeah. I've known her since we were knee high to a grasshopper."

"What?" I wrinkle my forehead.

Bradley shakes his head. "Get up. I'm getting you out of here."

Oddly enough, I obey without hesitation. It's like Bradley's the Ghost of Christmas Future, offering me a better life.

"Get your stuff." I turn toward the bathroom to collect my things. It's pitch black and I think I feel another roach. I decide I can live without whatever's over there and reach for my suitcase by the bed. Then I follow Bradley outside into the cold.

"Ouch." I hop across the sidewalk.

Bradley turns back. "Why aren't you wearing shoes?"

"You didn't give me time."

He shakes his head and continues walking. I scamper across the parking lot with frozen feet, toss my bag in the back of the patrol car, then climb inside. The engine is already running, so it's warm inside.

Bradley gets in and glances in the rearview mirror. "You don't have to sit back there."

"It's fine." I study the bars. "I've never been in the back of a cop car."

Bradley smiles. "One more reason you're better for Lacie than I ever was."

I return the smile and laugh, leaning back against the seat. A few miles down the road, the Christmas music is interrupted by a special weather report. Bradley turns up the volume, and I lean forward to listen better.

It's Jim Vann, the guy Lacie is obsessed with. He apologizes for underestimating the amount of snow in central Alabama, and predicts at least eight inches over the next day and a half.

I clap my hands and laugh.

"You like snow as much as Lacie, huh?"

"No. But she's been telling everyone for weeks this was coming. None of us believed her, not even her boss."

Bradley smiles into the mirror. "Good for her, then, huh?"

"Yep."

We pull up to a camper surrounded by pine trees. Bradley's red truck is parked out front. He turns off the engine. "Okay, you can stay with me tonight. It's not much, but I have an extra set of bunk beds. I texted my buddy Kyle. He's gonna pick up your car when it gets to be a decent hour. You can talk to him about either fixing it or hauling it back to Atlanta for you."

"The same Kyle from the cow-poop competition?"

Bradley smiles. "Yeah, that's the one. Best body shop guy around."

Thirty minutes ago, I'd have killed anyone who suggested I spend the night with Bradley. But he's actually being a decent guy right now, and my only other options are a wrecked puke-mobile covered in snow or a roach motel with no power or hot water.

I sigh as Bradley climbs out of the car. "Thanks."

He turns back and nods. "I really want this to work for you and Lacie. I think you two are right for each other."

I nod and open my own door. Then I pull a pair of shoes from my bag, because I can only imagine what's in Bradley's yard.

Lacie

A BRIGHT LIGHT shines through my window. I blink my eyes open and roll onto my back. I fell asleep with my curtain open so I could watch the snow fall. I decided I'd better enjoy it while it lasts. By the way my room's lit up now, there must not be a cloud in the sky.

I get up and walk to the window to check. My eyes nearly fall from their sockets when I realize the brightness is from a thick blanket of sparkly white snow on the ground. I stumble across the room to pull on a pair of boots and my coat, then I rush outside to the front porch. It's still cloudy, just not snowing currently. When I step off the porch into the yard, snow covers half my boot. I scream. I was so right!

I do a weird little dance in the yard. In my red polka-dot pajamas, Frye boots, and parka. Real cute, I'm sure. But I couldn't care less right now. When I turn to go inside, Mama and Liam are standing at the door, staring at me as if I've lost my mind.

"Mama, it snowed!"

"That's nice, honey." She smiles warmly. "Why don't you come have some breakfast casserole? It won't be long before we have to get down to G-Maw's for the hog killing."

"And the deer skinning," Liam adds.

"Son, we are not eating that roadkill. Your father said so."

Liam groans as he and Mama go back inside. I smile up at the sky once more and mouth a "thank you" toward heaven. Then I hop up the porch steps and go inside.

I leave my boots on the Frosty rug in front of the door and go to the kitchen. Liam and Daddy are already eating. "Merry Christmas, Daddy." He smiles over his coffee mug. "Merry Christmas, Lacie Bug."

I grab two coffee cups. One for me and one for Collins. Collins.

I freeze. What am I doing? Collins isn't here. I should

know this. He'd have been in my room, and I'd have been downstairs with Bully. I suck in a breath, then exhale.

A hand runs across my back. I glance over my shoulder, halfway hoping its him. It's Mama. "You okay, baby?"

"Yes, ma'am. Just sleepy."

She nods. "Aren't we all. That midnight service gets me every year."

I press my lips into a slight smile, then push one of the mugs back beside the coffeemaker. I fill my own mug and add some sweetener to it. With not much of an appetite, I lean against the countertop and gaze out the window. A few flurries begin to fall in the backyard.

Daddy notices the flurries, too. "Looks like we'll have to kill Myrtle in the barn. I don't want snow soggin' up the meat."

"It'll be fine. Cold weather is good for hog killing," Mama adds as she sits at the table with Daddy and Liam. "Aren't you going to eat, Lacie?"

I turn toward her and raise my eyebrows. "In a bit. I'm still waking up." Waking up to the realization that my life will now go on without Collins.

Maybe I should just call him. Rip the Band-aid. Call a truce. Forget all this "women are strong, he should call first," yada yada. I need to be alone for a few minutes.

"I'm going to get ready first." I announce my intentions so Mama will quit questioning me. Then I finish my coffee, set the cup in the sink, and go back to my room.

I shut the door and get back in bed. I'm actually not that tired or sleepy. Just blah. I allow myself a five-minute pity party, then I change into some older jeans and a T-shirt. I layer a sweatshirt over that, then pull my coveralls over everything and zip them up. This will make for a nice snowsuit.

Growing up in Alabama, I've only owned one actual snowsuit. I begged for one when I was like eight, because I was so obsessed with snow. I would wear it playing outside whenever it got cold, hoping snow would fall. It only flurried once before I outgrew it.

I put on a little bit of makeup, since random people around town show up for this occasion. The hog killing is the talk of the town each year and draws a lot of people from Apple Cart as well. I don't want gossiping people saying I've "let myself go" at age twenty-five.

I pull my hair into a ponytail, shove my phone in my coveralls pocket, and grab my old rubber boots from the closet. I return to the kitchen in my sock feet and set my boots by the island, then I cut a small piece of casserole. If I don't stick something solid in my mouth, Mama will shove a thermometer under my tongue or look up "loss of appetite" on WebMD. When I sit at the table with a plate of food, she grins at me.

I pick at my food and listen to Daddy lecture Liam on driving in the snow. Mama sips her coffee and gazes out the window. She likes the snow, too. I can see it in her eyes.

After Daddy runs out of ways Liam can wreck, he ends his speech with, "Let's load up." He and Liam head for the garage. I rake my leftovers in the trash and carry my plate to the sink. Mama stands and goes through her worrying routine of making sure each and every knob in the kitchen is switched off. Then she bundles up, too, and we go out into the garage.

Daddy has meticulously wrapped the knives and other equipment in towels and laid them on the back floorboard so as to not let any snow fall on them. I open the back door and stare at all the accessories.

"There's no room back here, I guess I'll have to drive." Liam shrugs and smiles.

"Nope. You can ride with Lacie. She has four-wheel drive," Daddy says.

I smirk at Liam. He rolls his eyes and trudges toward my Honda.

Daddy calls out after us, "Come over here first and help me load Myrtle."

Liam turns again and heads for the dog pen. I snicker as I run in the house and get my keys. When I come back outside, Liam is shoving Myrtle's butt up a ramp. I grab my phone and snap a picture for blackmail. At least they got the metal four-wheeler ramp this time. I swear, she looks even heavier than when we got her.

Once the pig is loaded, Liam hops over the tailgate and rubs his hands down the front of his pants. He jogs over to my car and opens the door. Once he's in the car, he starts to hold onto the dash.

"Don't touch anything."

He grins at me and hovers his hand over the radio.

"Not if you don't want this on Instagram." I tap on the pig butt photo and hold up my phone.

He reaches for it, but I let it fall by my feet. He swipes his pig butt hand across my face and chuckles.

"Ohhh." I growl at him and put my crossover in reverse. Why couldn't I be an only child like Collins? Oh, Collins. I sigh and pull out into the road behind Daddy's truck. Myrtle stares back at us, wiggling her snout. Poor pig doesn't know what's coming.

Earl's family, Woody, and Michael are standing around the barn when we pull up at G-Maw's. I park a safe distance from where the crime scene will take place. I learned better the year Misty's rowdy boys got in a fight with the discards, and pig guts landed on the hood of my car.

Earl and Michael come over to help unload the hog. I head for the house. I'm fine with killing a hog. I just don't want to watch it. Every year, I help G-Maw wash pans and prepare seasoning while the guys do the dirty work.

All of Misty's kids are now with their respective daddies except for Michael and Piper. Krystal is still here as well. She and Aunt Bea sit in the two recliners, rocking simultaneously. Aunt Bea is adding on to the tassel scarf, perhaps making it a blanket. Krystal is rubbing her belly.

"How are you feeling, Krystal?" I ask.

She curves the corners of her lips. "Pretty good. I couldn't sleep much last night."

I nod. "Maybe it was the weather."

"I don't know. My back's been bothering me."

I imagine it's the baby weighing her down. "Let me know if I can get you anything."

"Thanks." She leans her head against the recliner and sighs. I continue into the kitchen, where G-Maw is shaking various bottles of seasoning into a bowl. I give her a side hug. "Sorry I'm late. Daddy took his dear time packing the supplies."

G-Maw laughs. "Wonder where he gets that." She winks at me.

"Yeah, thanks for passing that on to me, too." I laugh, then wash my hands to help.

Michael dries and stacks some trays that G-Maw has washed, then heads toward the door. "Hey, Krystal, come on, honey, you'll want to see this."

I peek around the corner to watch Krystal waddle toward the front door. Michael helps ease her out onto the turf and shuts the door behind them.

"She's got a stronger stomach than me." I dry my hands and pop a lid on the bowl of spices before shaking it.

"Oh, you could get used to it, too, if you had to. Back when I was your age, folks killed their own food all the time. Ed and I started this tradition when your Mama was little to show our kids how easy they have it nowadays. And to show them all the hard work that people used to have to put in just to eat. Be thankful it's a tradition for you. For me, it was survival."

I smile at G-Maw, then puff my cheeks and exhale. Thank God, I was born in the 1990s. G-Maw and I work on different seasoning mixes and clean a few more pans as we chat about the snow, the hog, and everyday life.

"Did Collins have to go back to work?"

I swallow, not sure how to answer this. Might as well get it over with, though, so we can go on with our Christmas. "Well—"

A blood-curling scream comes from outside. G-Maw and I look at one another, then out the window. We can't see the barn from here. "Hold on." I place a hand on her arm for her to stay inside, and rush through the living room. Aunt Bea is still rocking and humming as if she didn't hear a thing. Which she probably didn't.

I bolt out the door, letting the screen slam shut behind me. Krystal is sitting on a stump, bowed over, crying. Michael rubs her back. "It's okay. I cried the first time I watched, too. I was four, but still."

Mama and Carla beat me to her. Mama puts the back of her hand to Krystal's forehead, then feels of her cheek. "Krystal, what's wrong?" I'm glad she doesn't have phone service out here, or she'd pull up WebMD.

Aunt Carla bends down and talks to her like she's her kindergarten teacher. "Sweetie, I'll go get you some water. Be brave, okay?"

I walk over and meet Mama's gaze. "Do you think she's in labor?"

Mama stands and lowers her voice. "She's not due for another month."

I shrug. "Yeah, but?"

Aunt Carla rushes up with some ice water. Krystal

screams again and kicks. Carla flinches and spills the water on Michael. "Sorry, son."

He shakes his head. "It's fine."

"No, it's not. It hurts!" Krystal yells again.

She's right. This isn't fine. "We need to get her to the hospital."

"I heard on the scanner all the main roads are closed. That's why none of the town folks are here," Earl chimes in, as if it's no big deal.

I wish Collins were here. He'd know what to do.

CHAPTER NINETEEN

Collins

I wake up to the smell of bacon. A much better greeting than I expected after the late night/early morning I had. I raise my head a little too quickly and knock it on the ceiling of the camper. "Oomph." I lean back on my elbow and rub my head. I was so tired at two o'clock that I didn't give much attention to the distance between the top bunk and the ceiling. Normally, I'd have chosen the bottom bunk, but sleeping low to the ground hadn't served me well in Wisteria.

I keep my head hunched and swing my legs over the side. Then I turn and make it down the ladder in two steps. It smells good in here, the place is clean, and Bradley didn't murder me in my sleep. So I'd say my situation is improving.

The bacon scent calls me toward the front of the camper. And while my nose is in heaven, I can't say the same for my eyes. I'm blinded by Bradley standing over the small stove in a pair of Santa briefs.

"Morning, buddy."

I blink and turn my eyes toward the kitchen window. "What time is it?"

"Ten. I let you sleep in. I'm gonna drive you over to Kyle's. He pulled your truck into his shop earlier. Then we can see about getting you to Lacie."

I suck in a breath and hold it.

"That sound like a plan?" he asks.

I turn to Bradley, making sure I keep my eyes level with his. "Are you sure Lacie will want to see me?"

Bradley points a spatula at me. "Yes, and as the authority around these parts, I'm not letting you leave Apple Cart County until you propose."

I frown, then turn back toward the bunks.

"I mean it, Collins."

"I heard you."

I sit on the bottom bunk and rummage through my suitcase for something that doesn't smell like the roach motel. I've got nothing, so I settle for the least wrinkled shirt and some pressed jeans. I have no clean socks, so I go with a pair that weren't worn in the shower or the streets.

After changing, I rummage through my suitcase for my toiletries. Then I remember I left them at the Quality Inn. Or just Inn. I should call and suggest they leave the lights out on Quality. Not that any of the lights were working when we left.

"Hey, Bradley, do you have any extra toothpaste and toothbrush and floss and deodorant?"

"Dude, you didn't pack none of that?"

I sigh. "I left it at the inn."

"You can use my toothpaste."

"How am I supposed to brush my teeth without a toothbrush?"

"I dunno, use your finger? And calm down, I'll drive you by DG before we see Lacie."

I shake my head. I guess I'll settle for bacon breath until then. I reach for my phone. It's dead. There's an outlet across from my bed, so I plug it in.

"Breakfast is ready." Bradley walks up with two plates of pancakes and bacon. He sets them on the table near my bed. "Come eat."

I scratch my chin and nod at him.

"Oh." He chuckles. "I'll pray."

I bow my head and stare at the floor while he prays. Once he's finished, I ask, "Could you please put on some pants?"

"Yeah, dude. Sorry." He walks past me, and I lift my head at the worst possible moment. I wince, then feel my way to the table without looking.

He returns a minute later, but I'm afraid to look. "I've lived by myself so long, I forget."

I squint one eye open to Bradley licking syrup from his finger. He's still shirtless, but he has on pants, so I open my eyes fully. "Want some?" He shoves a giant bottle of syrup with an eagle on it toward me.

"Sure." I allow him to pour some on my pancakes. I take a bite. "Wow, this is good. I've never had that syrup before."

"Yeah, it's kinda local."

After we finish eating, Bradley stands and takes the plates to the sink. "Let me text Kyle, and we can head that way."

"Okay." I go to my own phone and check it. I have three missed calls. All recent, from the same number. It's a 787 number, so it must be local.

"Hey, Bradley, do you know whose number is 787-2239?"

"Yeah, that's G-Maw's house phone."

I run a hand over my hair. "Why would G-Maw call my phone?"

"Maybe it was Lacie."

But why wouldn't she use her cell phone? I shrug, then notice there's one voicemail. A breathless Lacie is on the other end of the line. She sounds panicky, but I'm able to understand enough to realize Krystal is in labor. I hang up the phone.

"Uh, Bradley. Can we go to G-Maw's before Kyle's?" I peek around the corner, happy to see he's now fully dressed.

"I know you want to patch things up with Lacie, but Kyle's going to his grandparents' house at noon."

"This isn't about Lacie. I've got to deliver a baby."

"Oh." Bradley's eyes bug, and he hurries out of the camper. "Let's go." He grabs his hat out of his cop car and hops in the truck. I jump in the truck and shudder at the thought of any cat dander lingering on the seat. Surely, it's gone by now.

Bradley reaches under his seat and pulls out one of those police lights that attaches to a regular car. He puts it on the top of the truck and turns it on, then he screeches out of his drive, slinging gravel and snow in every direction.

I buckle as fast as I can and hold onto any and all handles I can find. Nobody is on the road right now, and for good reason. Bradley turns on his CB radio, and we hear reports about the weather and all the major roads being closed.

I fumble around with my phone and try to call Lacie, but her phone just keeps ringing. I try and call G-Maw's number, but it's busy. Finally, I give up trying to call and pray that we make it there in time.

Lacie

AFTER KRYSTAL SCREAMED for the fourth time, Mama and Carla suggested we move her to the back bedroom. They kept saying things like "it's Braxton-Hicks" and "I bet the baby's on her sciatic nerve." But no matter what it was, we all thought it best she go and lie down. Of course, the men liked this better, too. All of her screaming was putting a damper on their hog killing.

Michael and Daddy carried her inside. Then Daddy left to resume his job as head meat slicer. Mama went to boil water, and Aunt Carla brought her some ice water and extra pillows. G-Maw went to her prayer closet. Meanwhile, I tried to call all the doctors in town. Dr. Newhart was at the hospital in Tuscaloosa, which was where we'd love to be right now but couldn't. Dr. Deerman was on a Christmas cruise with his family. At least, according to his Facebook profile, since nobody answered the phone at his home or office.

That left the only other doctor I knew who might be close. Collins. Most likely, he drove all night to beat the snow and is now in Atlanta living his best life. But I owed it to Krystal to try. So I called three times. On the last attempt, I left a desperate voicemail. I didn't mention anything about us, or even me, just Krystal and the baby.

Regardless of how he feels about me and my family, we need him right now.

Dr. Newhart's wife had said we could call the hospital with any questions. I've called a few times, as none of us have delivered a baby before. That is, unless you count that G-Maw had Uncle Earl at home. But she was the one pushing, not pulling.

I'm picking up the phone to call the hospital once more when a police siren bellows outside. Very strange, since nobody has been on the road for hours. And it's now snowing much heavier than before.

The siren gets louder, then stops completely. Weird. I turn my finger in the rotary dial, which is a pain with the area code included. Next year, G-Maw's getting a cordless, push-button phone from me.

As I half listen to the instrumental Christmas music playing on the other end of the line, the front door bursts open. It's Collins . . . and Bradley . . . together? I don't even care. I drop the phone and run to Collins.

"You came." I wrap my arms around his neck and suck in his scent. Expect it's not *his* scent. Instead of masculine after-shave, he smells like cigarette smoke and syrup. But I don't care.

"Where is she?"

My smile fades, and I drop back from him when I remember that he's here for Krystal. And only Krystal. "Back bedroom, come on." I grab his hand and lead him to the back of the house. I swallow and warn myself not to get too giddy about holding his hand. It's all professional now.

Krystal lies in the center of the bed with every pillow in the house surrounding her. She looks like a MyPillow infomercial. Collins drops my hand and rushes to the side of the bed. My nerves zap when his touch is gone, but I make myself focus on Krystal. If the roles were reversed, I wouldn't want her pining for my doctor's attention.

Collins immediately gives Mama and Carla a list of items he needs. Then he tells me all the medications that are safe for her to take for pain that G-Maw might have on hand. We scatter throughout the house like a football team breaking from the huddle. Kinda like we did before, except this time we have a quarterback. And we're all perfectly content to let Collins take the ball and run with it, as G-Maw would say.

The good thing about Michael having a one-year-old

sister is that we have instant access to diapers and formula. Of course, the diapers will be more like a Spanx on the newborn, but we'll make do with what we've got.

Michael stays by Krystal, helping her sip water and adjusting pillows at her command. I bring Collins the medicine I found, including one he didn't list. He stares at the bottle. "These are opioids."

"That will work, right?"

"Yeah, it will work." He takes the bottle from me and raises his brows as he reads the label. "These were G-Maws?"

"Yeah, from when she got her hip replacement. She only took one or two, but G-Paw put the rest in the gun safe. He said if they ever fell on hard times, he could sell them."

Collins shrugs. "I suppose he could." He hands the bottle to Michael. "Have her take one of these. It's not as good as an epidural, but it'll help calm her down."

Michael nods and helps Krystal swallow the pill. Mama and Carla return from their respective assignments. Collins puts a damp cloth across Krystal's forehead and talks to her about the delivery.

The medicine starts to kick in, and Krystal gets calmer. She complains about some back pain and shifts around. After one particular painful spell, Collins checks and announces that it's time. Carla closes the door. She and Mama stand on either side of Krystal to assist Collins. Michael stays by her head, stroking her hair and telling her to focus on him and not what's going on below. It seems to work, though I'm not sure I'd be able to do the same.

I sit in the corner and twist a lock of my hair until it almost falls out of my head. There's a reason I'm not a medical person. I've avoided watching a hog slaughter today, so why ruin my streak by watching someone give birth? I hug my knees in front of my face and pray everything goes well.

After another loud scream from Krystal, everyone starts

to cheer. I hear a baby cry, and Collins announce it's a girl. He then instructs Michael on cutting the umbilical cord. I wait a few minutes, then peek over my kneecap. Carla is wrapping the baby in a sheet and handing her to Krystal.

I slide up the wall to standing. Michael and Krystal kiss each other, then the baby. Their faces glow with happiness. Well, happiness and sweat for Krystal. Mama and Carla are arm in arm with one another, crying. They both love babies. Collins wipes his hands as he heads to the master bathroom connected to the bedroom.

I slip behind everyone and go to the bathroom. He's standing at the vanity, washing his hands. "You were great," I say.

He looks in the mirror and smiles back at me. "Thanks. I've never delivered a baby before."

"Thank God, you got my message. We couldn't get to the hospital in time, and none of the local doctors were available."

Collins turns off the faucet and dries his hands. "I'm glad you called. I would've come sooner, but my phone was dead."

I nod. My whole body tingles as I stand in front of him. I want to run into his arms and kiss him, but I hold back. Just because he came back and helped my family doesn't mean we're back together. It doesn't undo him leaving. Since I'm not sure where we stand, I go ahead and bring up the elephant in the room.

"I was surprised to see you with Bradley."

"Yeah, so was I. He kind of rescued me last night."

"Rescued you?" I lower myself to sitting on the edge of the tub and stare at him.

Collins tosses the towel in the sink and sighs. "It's a long story, but I hit a tree on my way out of town—or rather a tree hit me—wrecked the Land Rover, and needed a place to stay."

"Oh." I stare at the shag rug under my feet.

"Lacie, I'm sorry I left. When I saw you kiss Bradley, I thought you wanted to get back with him."

"Whoa." I jump to my feet. This explains so much, but I can't let him think I wanted that kiss. "I didn't want to, I—"

He raises a hand to shush me. "I know, Bradley explained. It's all his fault, and I know that. I was insecure, and I got scared and left. It was a cowardly thing to do, and I'm sorry."

My defenses start to melt. Collins smiles at me, and I step forward to hug him. But before I can, he drops down on his knee and reaches in his pocket. He pulls out a little black box and opens it.

I stare down at the most beautiful antique diamond I've ever seen. I swallow hard and blink to make sure this isn't a dream. I'm wearing rubber boots and coveralls unzipped to my waist, and we're standing in the middle of G-Maw's bathroom. Not how I pictured this moment at all. Maybe this is a dream.

"Lacie, you know I love you. What you don't know is that I came to Wisteria with the intentions of proposing to you on Christmas Eve."

I hold my chest to try and slow my heart rate. All this time, Collins had planned on proposing, and I had no idea.

"I wanted to get to know your parents, ask your dad's permission, and find a romantic spot to propose. None of that went as planned. But I can't go back to Atlanta without knowing we'll spend the rest of our lives together. I haven't asked your dad, and I know we're in the bathroom . . ." Collins peers around at the ceramic butterflies and floral wall paper. "But I'm tired of waiting for the right time. Before anymore wrecks, or babies or hogs interfere, I need to know, will you marry—"

I should've probably let him finish. But I couldn't stand

there any longer. I leap into his arms and kiss him. He wraps his arms around me and kisses me back. We sit there for a long time, hugging, kissing, and laughing in G-Maw's bathroom. He slides the ring on my finger, and we laugh and hug some more. We might've stayed there the rest of the day had someone not knocked on the door.

Collins stands and opens it. Aunt Misty's youngest boy stares up at us. "Sorry, but G-Maw said I can't pee outside when we have company." I want to tell him there's another bathroom, but don't. We've got to come out and face reality sometime.

"Oh, okay." Collins grins at me, then takes my hand and leads me out. Time to make our debut as an engaged couple.

CHAPTER TWENTY

Collins

Lacie and I walk out into the bedroom. Michael sits on the edge of the bed beside Krystal as they admire their daughter. I walk over to them and smile. "You both did great."

Michael raises his head and grins. "No, man, you did great."

"Thanks, I'm glad I could help. This was a first for me, too. Krystal, I'll have Lacie call the hospital. As soon as the roads clear enough, you and the baby need to go in for a checkup with your doctor."

She nods. "Of course."

"We'll give you two some privacy."

Krystal nods again and smiles. Then she raises her head off the pillow and smiles even wider. "Lacie, is that a new ring?"

Lacie blushes and holds out her hand. "Collins just gave it to me."

Krystal wiggles to see better. Then she holds her side and grunts. Michael puts a hand on her shoulder. "Take it easy."

Lacie steps closer to give her a better look.

"Oh, Lacie, that's gorgeous."

"Thanks." Lacie beams. I stand behind her and wrap my hands around her waist. I can hardly believe we're engaged. Finally.

"When's the wedding?" Michael looks up from the baby, all smiles.

"We don't know yet. This literally happened like ten minutes ago," Lacie says.

Michael nods. Krystal bats her eyelashes at him. "Are you thinking what I'm thinking?"

"That someone needs to take the back roads to DG for some smaller diapers?"

"No." Krystal wavers her head. "I mean, maybe soon, but I was actually thinking the four of us could have a double wedding."

Lacie's face goes pale. I clear my throat, wracking my brain for an answer to this crazy suggestion. "We appreciate the invitation, Krystal. But I think it would be more special for all of us if we had our own weddings."

Lacie leans back on me and relaxes her shoulders.

Krystal's jaw drops a little at first, then she goes back to grinning. "You're right. I wouldn't want to outshine Lacie in my mermaid gown."

"Thank you, Krystal. That's so considerate." Lacie feigns a smile, then smirks at me. "We'll leave you two alone to feed the baby."

"Okay, congrats again." Michael waves as we start to leave.

We walk out of the bedroom and shut the door. The house is quiet, so I assume everyone is outside. Except for

Aunt Bea. She's rocking and humming in the living room when we pass by.

"Look, for the baby." We turn back to see her holding up what was the scarf with tassels but is now the size of a baby blanket. However, it still has the tassels.

"That's great, Aunt Bea." Lacie smiles at her, then turns back to me. "I had no idea she even knew what was going on."

I shrug. "Maybe she pays more attention than we thought."

We continue outside, and Lacie pulls her arms into her coveralls and zips them up. I glance over and admire my grandma's ring on her finger. I've waited a long time for that.

"Hey, guys." Earl Ed greets us on the porch. "We've got bacon." He holds up a piece and folds it into his mouth.

Lacie laughs. "Thanks, maybe later."

"Let's find your parents."

She nods. We go to the edge of the yard, where Mr. and Mrs. Sanderson are standing by his truck tailgate, eating their own bacon and fixings.

Lacie's face lights up when they notice us standing there. "Mama, Daddy, I have news." She lifts her hand and wiggles her fingers. Her mom leaps toward us and engulfs Lacie.

I'm more worried about Mr. Sanderson, as he's not reacting in any way. "Sir, I wanted to ask your permission. I'd come here planning to do that, but everything kept happening and all, and—"

He extends his hand, causing me to stop. I stare at it a moment before shaking it. He grins. "I understand. Lacie is a grown woman, and we trust her judgment. I've enjoyed getting to know you this week. Anyone who can put up with this family deserves a trophy. And I can't think of a better trophy than my daughter."

"Agreed." I laugh.

He pulls me closer for one of those half-hugs men do where we pat each other's backs then release. "Welcome to the family, Collins."

"Thanks, Mr. Sanderson."

"Please, son, call me Mr. Joey."

"Mr. Joey." I smile. Still formal, but he's definitely warming up to me calling him Joey.

"My baby's getting married." I guess Mrs. Sanderson—or should I now say Mrs. Robin—can't contain her excitement any longer.

With her declaration, everyone gathers from their respective places around the barn to come congratulate us. G-Maw wraps her arms around my waist and hugs me tightly. "I had a good feeling about you, boy."

"Thanks, G-Maw."

Earl walks up all solemn and hands me a gun. "An early wedding present. Welcome to the family."

I stare at the rifle for a long moment, then meet Earl's eyes. "Thanks."

"You'll need it in this family." He winks, then chuckles. "And we'd love to have you join us at the Alabama Gun Club banquet next month. With Lacie as your plus one, of course."

"They can sit at the head table by me," Bradley spouts off around a mouthful of pig.

"Why not?" I raise my hands and smile. I'm no longer threatened by Bradley. It's obvious that Lacie loves me and that everyone's in agreement that we should be married.

We all migrate toward the barn, where the food is set up. There're two separate fire pits where Mr. Joey and Earl are cooking the food, and another smaller fire for us to sit around. G-Maw heads back in the house to see the baby and check on Aunt Bea, while the rest of us eat meat and pig cookies. Which are not cookies from the actual pig. Carla made pink sugar cookies decorated like pig heads and pig backsides. They're really good.

I sit in front of the fire with my arm around Lacie. We all listen as Bradley strums something on a guitar. Of course, he'd know how to play the guitar. But I let this one slide. I delivered a baby today, thank you very much.

On my way into town, I'd imagined us celebrating the engagement in a white wooden gazebo with Christmas lights and hot chocolate. Not in a rusty metal barn with heat lamps and bacon. But in the end, all that matters is that Lacie and I get to spend the rest of our lives together.

Lacie

I FINISH SWIPING on my mascara and reach for my lip gloss. As I rub the stick across my lips, my ring twinkles in the bathroom mirror. I smile as excitement runs through my body. I can hardly believe we're engaged.

After the hog killing, Bradley took Collins and me to check on the Land Rover at Kyle's. We decided to let him fix it since he could beat any price in Atlanta. Plus, Kyle does great work. The next morning, the sun popped out and the roads began to melt. The county started salting all the country roads where the trees shaded the paths. By noon, the major roads were open, and we could go home. Kyle promised to deliver the Land Rover ASAP, so we headed back to Atlanta in my crossover.

On the way home, Collins told me the whole story of how he ended up with Bradley on Christmas. Everything from the wreck on Broken Bridge to the power outage at

Quality Inn. I laughed so hard that I choked on my Starbucks, which we bought as soon as we got to Tuscaloosa. I'd had serious withdrawals drinking Piggly Wiggly creamer.

I hate that he wrecked . . . again. But I am thankful that he couldn't make it home before finding out the truth of what happened when Bradley kissed me. And I'm really thankful that he was there to help Krystal.

As we were leaving, Earl Ed was preparing to take Michael, Krystal, and the baby to the hospital.

I Venmo'd Mama some money to get them a playpen from Collins and me. I learned the hard way never to Venmo Aunt Misty. Last spring, I sent her thirty dollars to get Piper a cute outfit for Easter, and she used it to buy a new Dolly Parton wig.

I run a brush through my hair and check my appearance in the mirror. I raise and lower my shoulders, then turn out the light and head for the front of my apartment. I'm more excited than usual about work today. Since I was there last, I've gotten engaged and the snowstorm manifested over central Alabama, just as I'd predicted.

I leave a few minutes early so I can run into Starbucks on my way. You know, for good luck. By the time I'm at my building, my latte is gone. High on caffeine and happiness, I float into my cubicle and start getting ready for the day.

"Lacie?"

I twist in my chair to see my boss standing in the open space of my cubicle wall.

"Hi, Mark."

"Can I talk to you for a minute?"

"Sure." I push my chair back and follow Mark into his office.

He sits behind his desk and smooths his tie against his chest. "I want to be the first to congratulate you."

I smile and stare down at my hands in my lap. I raise my

left hand and wiggle my fingers. That's been my new favorite gesture the last few days.

"Oh, wow. Did you get engaged?"

I nod excitedly.

"Congratulations. The surgeon?"

"Yes."

"Cool." He clears his throat and steeples his fingers. I drop my hand, since I now feel silly dangling it in the air as if I'm giving spirit fingers at a cheer competition.

"Wait, so if you didn't know about the ring, then . . .?"

"Congratulations on getting promoted to co-host the *Weird Weather Hour*."

It's a good thing I put my hand down, because it's now shaking. My jaw drops.

"That is, if you want it. I know you've expressed interest in becoming a show host. And we were really impressed with your prediction of the snowstorm in Alabama."

By some miracle, I manage to unhinge my jaw and find my voice. "Of course, I'd love to."

Mark offers me a rare smile. I return it.

"We'll start interviewing for your job, then. You can guest host a few times until then, but the job is yours as soon as we find your replacement."

I sit there with a stupid grin plastered across my face, unable to speak again. I know my grin is stupid because of the face Mark makes back to me. "I'll give you more details as we go. Now, go do your current job."

I bob my head a little too enthusiastically and scurry back to my cubicle. According to Dustin, I gave my best on-camera reporting ever after that news. Well, except for the fact that I slid into a southern accent on a few words. He was so kind as to show me that clip over and over when we got back to the office. What can I say? Wisteria will rub off on a person.

After a long day of catching up, I sit in traffic, watching the sun set. It's literally that slow. When I finally get home, I call Collins to tell him the news. As I walk up to my apartment door, I hear his voice echoing. I hold my phone out, assuming it's bad reception.

I gasp as someone grabs me. When I see Collin's watch and scrub sleeves, I relax. "You scared me." I elbow him, and he holds onto his side.

"You hurt me."

"You deserve it." I narrow my eyes at him. He laughs and releases me to open the door. Once we're inside he asks, "What's for dinner?"

"Cereal or whatever G-Maw made us bring home, your pick."

He snickers, then rubs his hands together as if he's up to something. "I thought we'd go out to celebrate our engagement."

I place my purse and keys on the counter and point to the refrigerator. "You sure?"

He smirks. "I'm sure."

"Do I need to change?"

"No, you look great. Just let me step out and grab my clothes to change."

I wrinkle my brow as he goes out and returns a few seconds later with a duffle bag.

"Wow, so you have everything planned. Did you have Charlie drop you off?"

"Nope. I took MARTA from the hospital. And I've never been more ready to get my vehicle back."

I laugh and put my arms around his neck. "Well, I've never been more ready for us to get married."

He gives me a quick kiss. "Same."

"And we have one more reason to celebrate."

"What's that?"

"I'll tell you over dinner."

He tilts his head at me, then bends down to pick up his bag. "Please tell me you didn't agree to that double wedding with Krystal and Michael."

I give him my best crazy laugh as he heads into the bedroom to change. We're in for one fun life together.

EPILOGUE

Six Months Later

Lacie

I stare down at my manicured nails and swallow.

Adrianne sticks a few more bobby pins in my hair, then bends down to see my face.

"You okay, honey?"

I lift my head and nod. "I'm just nervous. Collins and I have a history of crazy things happening, so I can only imagine what might go wrong.

"Cover your eyes." Adrianne sprays yet another layer of hairspray on my curls. "There. Now, look. You're gorgeous. Nothing will go wrong."

I sigh. "We'll see."

"Hey." She points the sharp end of a comb at me. "I've never gotten married, but I've been to a LOT of weddings. I've seen cakes dropped and dresses stepped on. I've seen flower girls cry and bridesmaids fall. But no matter what, the couple got married all the same. That's what matters." She picks at a few of my curls with the end of the comb. "You just focus on that sweet, handsome guy of yours, and it will all work out. 'Kay?"

I smile into the mirror, and she smiles back. "Okay."

"Now, let's get you to the altar."

I stand and hold a hand to my stomach. Butterflies swim in my gut as I try and focus on the good. Adrianne holds up my train and follows me through Aunt Carla's house. Once we're at the kitchen, she spreads the train. Then she steps in front of me and fans some locks of hair around my shoulders. "There. Like the cover of a wedding magazine." She curves her bright red lips and nods.

We stand in silence for a moment, listening to Bradley sing "I Will Always Love You." I close my eyes, focus on the guitar chords, and imagine Collins's reaction when I walk out. My perfect vision is quickly interrupted by a raspy female voice taking over the lyrics. I pop my eyes open and glare out the glass door. Aunt Misty has taken the mic. Bradley keeps playing while staring at her, not knowing what he should do.

Adrianne rests her hand on my shoulder. I flinch at her warm palm on my nervous skin. "It doesn't matter, honey. Just breathe."

I suck in, then exhale. "You're right. At least she's not dressed like Dolly."

Adrianne rubs my shoulder and grins. "That's the spirit." The music changes, and she pulls her hand from my shoulder. When she does, her rings take a thread with them. A strand of beads bounces to the tile floor. I cut my eyes toward her and frown.

"Minor flaw, honey." She hides the thread under my strap and twists another curl around to hide the bare satin by my neckline.

Before my nerves can tighten any more, the French doors to the patio open. The microphone screeches as Bradley snatches it from Misty and turns it off. Good for him.

Daddy comes down the aisle from seating Mama and steps up beside me. He kisses me on the cheek. "You look beautiful, Lacie Bug."

"Thanks, Daddy." I fight back tears as his own eyes moisten.

Once Mama sits, Bradley and the piano player transition to the wedding march. I watch Collins and Charlie step up to the arch of flowers and stand beside Brother Billy.

One by one, the wedding party meet, lock arms, and walk down the aisle. Liam and Carly are last to walk out. Carly holds her bouquet with one hand and leads Piper with the other. She's walking great now, but not quite sure what to do with her own flowers. Everyone oohs and aahs at her cuteness.

Bradley hits a chord that ramps up the music, and Brother Billy lifts his palms, signaling everyone to stand. All eyes turn to me. My stomach knots more times than an Eagle Scout can undo. I puff out my cheeks, then exhale one last time. This is it. Don't. Fall. Down.

Out of the corners of my eyes, I catch a glimpse of people smiling at me as Daddy leads me to the arch. But I'm focused on Collins and his face full of joy. He locks eyes with me and gives me the biggest smile I've ever seen. Well, except for maybe when he proposed in G-Maw's bathroom.

We stop in front of Brother Billy, and Daddy kisses my

cheek. When I notice tears in his eyes, I start to sniffle. I haven't seen my daddy cry since the day Liam declared he was going to Auburn over UA.

Daddy joins Mama in the front row of seats, and I somehow manage to suck in my tears. Collins smiles at me like I'm the most beautiful woman in the world. My heart speeds up, and I find it hard to focus as we recite our vows. But I know every bit of what they mean, and I mean every bit of them.

Brother Billy asks Collins to kiss his bride. As we lean in for a quick kiss, several people cheer and whistle. I refuse to look, but I can distinctly identify Aunt Misty and Earl Ed's voices. And I'm pretty sure that was Uncle Earl whistling. We hold hands and start down the aisle, everyone now cheering for us.

The reception is set up nearby around the patio. We barely make it to the cake when my wedding coordinator rushes up to me, clipboard in hand. Carolina clinches her teeth and frowns. "I'm so sorry about your aunt. Had I known she'd—"

I lift my hand and laugh. "It's not your fault. Nobody can predict Aunt Misty. Besides, we're married just the same." I smile up at Collins, and he kisses my cheek.

Carolina relaxes her shoulders. "Thank you."

"No, thank you." I motion around at the candles floating in the pool and the strands of lights above the patio. "You decorated and coordinated everything to a tee."

Carolina reaches out and hugs me. I wrap my arms around her and laugh. She pulls back when we hear Jonah call her name.

"Hey, Carol?"

"Yeah?"

"I think some of G-Maw's goats made it over here."

Jonah nods in the direction of the arch. Sure enough, two goats are chowing down on the flowers.

"Oh no. Come help me get them out of here." Carolina grabs Jonah and bolts toward the arch.

"At least they didn't get to the cake," Collins says.

I laugh. "Good point."

Jack walks by with a huge plate of food. Collins catches him by the arm. "Hey, man, thanks again for putting my family and Lacie's friends up at your place."

Jack licks his fingertips and shrugs. "No, thank you. Summers are slow for me, anyhow."

"Maybe you should offer some summer activities. They sure enjoyed it out there."

Jack raises his eyes, then nods at Collins as if he's never considered offering the lodge to anyone other than hunters before. "I might look into that."

"Thanks again, Jack," I say, smiling at him.

He nods again. "Anytime, Lacie."

Collins's groomsmen had gotten a room in Tuscaloosa, which worked well since they had his bachelor night in town. But his parents and my two Atlanta bridesmaids wanted to stay closer, so I asked Jack if they could rent the lodge. I didn't want to subject my in-laws and friends to the Quality Inn. Or just Inn, since they never got around to changing out the bulbs in "Quality." Probably a good call to not warrant false advertisement.

More and more people come our way, congratulating us and wishing us well. As I'm chatting with one of my old teachers, I catch a glimpse of Paul making his way through the food line, even though he wasn't invited. Oh well, who cares at this point.

As the sun sets, Bradley pulls the cop car around. The wedding planning had come together easily, except for how we'd leave. Collins joked one night that we could have

Bradley drive us away in the back of the cop car. That led to ten minutes of straight laughter. Then Collins mentioned it to Bradley, and he said he'd be honored. I don't think he gets Collins's dry sense of humor.

Everyone blows bubbles our way as we cram into the backseat. Bradley shuts us in and turns on the blue lights as we head down Uncle Earl's driveway. Once we reach the main road, he turns off the lights and drives to a side road where we've hidden my crossover, so Liam and Earl Ed couldn't find it. Otherwise, they'd have put sardines in the tailpipes and shaving cream on the windshield.

Bradley parks and grins into the rearview mirror. "Feel free to take those handcuffs as a wedding present." He winks at Collins.

Collins snarls his nose at the handcuffs laying by his feet. "Why don't you keep those? I have a feeling you'll need them sooner than me."

"All right, big dog. See y'all on Christmas, if not before."

We say our goodbyes as we climb out of the cop car and get into mine. I smile at Collins, happy that despite all the crazy in our lives, we're finally married.

We've come through so much in the last year and a half we've been together. And in the last six months, we've gotten engaged, he's gotten close to my family, and we've picked out a home together.

When we get back from the honeymoon, we can literally go home. Not to my hometown or simply to Atlanta, but to our own house in the suburbs. And it isn't the house that makes it home, just like growing up in Wisteria wasn't what made it my home. I now realize that home is where you belong. It's where your people are.

And Collins is my person.

Sign up for Kaci Lane's newsletter to receive a bonus scene of Michael and Krystal's wedding!

IF YOU ENJOYED *Christmas in Dixie*, check out other books I've written here. I'd also love it if you left a review to help other readers find my books.

ACKNOWLEDGMENTS

First, I'd like to thank God for giving me creative ideas and placing the right people in my path to help see them to fruition.

My husband, Blake, gets credit next for always supporting my writing endeavors, even if he finds my stories a little too "girly and Hallmarkish." Of course, this book kind of broke the mold when it comes to that.

I also want to thank several friends who helped me with fact checking. As well as author friends who encouraged me to go forward with such a quirky project. And I can't forget my college buddy, Courtney, who helped me brainstorm some of the fun, redneck rituals in this story.

Of course, I'd like to thank my editor, Joanne. She's always a pleasure to work with and polishes my books to help them shine.

ABOUT THE AUTHOR

Kaci Lane is a journalist turned fiction writer who believes all stories should have a happy ending. While unsuccessfully trying to learn Spanish for a decade, she has become fluent in sarcasm, Southern belle and movie quotes. She is married to a Southern Gentleman and has two young children who help keep her humility in check. Connect with her on kacilane.com or Facebook.

BOOKS BY KACI LANE

Schooled on Love Series

Taco Truck Takedown

Side Hustle

Buggy List

Off-Season

No Brides Club Series

No Time for Traditions

Coming Soon . . .

Bama Boys Series*

Hunting for Love

*If you enjoyed *Christmas in Dixie*, follow Kaci Lane for the upcoming Bama Boys series, starting in 2022 with *Hunting for Love*. Set in Apple Cart, Alabama, it includes secondary characters from *Christmas in Dixie*.